Buried Conscience

Glenn McLernon

Buried Conscience

This is a work of fiction. All characters and places and incidents are the product of the author's imagination.

First published in 2022 by Glenn McLernon, Hampshire, England.
e.mail gmclernon@googlemail.com
phone 07503184650 (UK)

Cover image: Mike Pellinni/Shutterstock.com

An electronic version of this work has been sent to the British Library.

ISBN: 978-0-9929145-9-2

Part One

They called it *The Alamo,* because of John Wayne's film. The ancient disused farm building, its crumbling, whitewashed walls sulking through the trees, seemed to spy out across the meadow. This ancient land had its secrets. Further on, through the trees, the woods and some boggy wetlands kept some old secrets too. A single railway line, still boasting the last of the majestic, puffing steam engines, cut through the countryside, separating the woodland and the wetland from a shimmering lake.

The *Alamo's* walls, last whitewashed decades before, stood crumbling and moss-stained. What had once been windows and doors were now untidy gaping holes. A few rotting skeletal beams were all that remained of the roof which, in some other age, proudly displayed a straw thatch. The floors had long since rotted away with weeds and scrub now growing here and there in unruly clumps in the rubble.

Pete Murphy crouched behind one of the gaping windows, his rifle resting on the loosening masonry and aimed out across the meadow at a point on the distant hedgerow. Squinting, he steadied himself and squeezed the trigger. The bang was accompanied by a sulphurous whiff with a curl of pale blue smoke. Emboldened, Pete moved from behind the wall and in quick succession fired several shots into the ranks of the *advancing enemy*.

Pete's offensive was cut short as he froze, his rifle fell from his hands, and he clutched his chest. He stumbled around for a few seconds, fear and pain on his face, uttering a few dying words to his comrade. "They got me, Jim." Then he fell, face down onto a heap of dry manure.

Jim Bowie crouched over his wounded comrade. "God damnit *Crockett*! You can't leave us now." But he hadn't noticed the *Mexican sniper* sneaking along the walls of the *Alamo* to lurk dangerously in the shadows. With a glint of a rifle barrel in the afternoon sun, the cowardly enemy took aim and with the time-honoured words … *bang, bang, you're dead, Jim Bowie* bit the dust or rather, the manure heap. As he fell, his face knocked against *Davy Crockett's* right foot, sending blood streaming from his nose. The *Mexican* stood triumphant over the conquered *Gringos*.

"I claim zis territory for Mehico. You are my prisoners … Dogs!"

The *Gringos* pulled the *Mexican* onto the manure heap and the three boys wrestled like tiger cubs at play.

George had to stop cavorting when his nose bled again. He sat-up on the dirt, his head tilted back with blood streaming from his nose.

"I'm going to see that film again." Said Pete Murphy.

"Yeh, when?" Said Alfie Dawes. (The Mexican).

"Saturday. The last showing.... Ya comin."

Alfie and George Murray both shook their heads at the same time.

"Naw, no doe." Said Alfie. "Ya lucky begger. The Alamo was the best film ever. D'ya remember the song?"

Pete began to hum. "A time just for livin ..... a time just for lovin ..... mmm.... Don't know all the words. Brilliant though!"

The three boys lay there in their exhilarated silence, savouring another long warm, school-free summer day.

"There's an over eighteen flick too." Said Pete.

"Bet ya won't get in." George mumbled as he nursed his bloody nose.

Pete laughed.... "Betya I will."

"Anyone got any fags?" Alfie said, trying to sound grown up.

Pete jumped to his feet and moved over to what had once been a window. He slid a stone away from its home, to reveal a hole where he had stashed a cigarette packet.

"Only got two left. You guys'll hav'ta share." He said, trying to sound like John Wayne.

He struck a match along the wall, just like in all the best cowboy pictures.

Pete was slightly taller than the others with thick hair which fell in an unruly fringe above his mischievous blue eyes. He was a natural leader. George had a kinder way about him, but he could be as cheeky as Pete. He had the knack of avoiding trouble. Then there was little Alfie, the ginger haired kid. His skin always seemed so milky white through the brown freckles, the exposed parts turning a bright pink when the sun was strong. Alfie followed the pack nervously, usually getting the blame when the other two had long scarpered.

They sucked on the Sweet Afton cigarettes which Pete had nicked from the glovebox of his father's car, an Austin Cambridge. Choking; Alfie coughed. He felt dizzy and sick.

"Holy cow! They're strong. Where did ya get 'em?"

"Ain't sayin." Said Pete and he spat at the wall as if he were a cowboy chewing tobacco.

Alfie looked at the blob of spit, which was making a trail as it ran down the wall. He was envious of Pete, wishing he could spit like him. Pete spat fast and accurate, as if he could spit like a gun, firing bullets. There seemed to be a knack to it. Alfie worked the saliva in his mouth and when he had enough spit, he jolted his head forward and spat the mouthful at the wall. It landed well below Pete's spit, almost at the ground. George took his turn. His bloodied spit didn't even make it to the wall. Pete laughed.

"How d'ya do that?" Alfie said.

Pete assumed a superior posture. "Easy." He said, puckering his lips and firing another bullet of spit at the wall.

The puerile competition went on until the wall was covered with streams of bubbly saliva, disgusting to an adult but to three boys playing in their fort it was more like a chart of manhood.

The *Alamo* was supposed to be out of bounds. It was on Josh Cogan's land. Josh seemed ancient to the boys, but he was really only about fifty, if that. He went about in a worn-out grey suit which had been relegated from Sunday best to a spare suit and finally earning its keep as work clothes. A few grey chest hairs sprung out at the top of his collarless shirt and a permanent stubble, fuzzed greyish around his chin. A well fingered brown trilby never left his head, while his hobnail boots covered his *hobnail feet.*

Josh owned about three hundred acres of the most fertile farmland. The locals would gossip about him and about his wealth. *Money to burn and no one to spend it on.... He still has his Communion money....* they would say. His house was called Caqueux House, and the boys swore it was haunted. A scrawny old woman, known only as Meg, served as Josh's housekeeper. She lived in the semi basement rooms at Cagueux House. The boys had always thought that Meg was married to Josh. They were afraid her, often swapping stories about how she would capture children and lock them in her *haunted, rat-infested* cellar.

The boys thought that no one knew about the *Alamo* being their hideout. It was their special secret place where they were free; free to experiment with life, although they were unaware that that was what they were actually doing. Here they could indulge in smoking and puerile talk about girls, farting and spitting competitions. From their base they would make *raids* into the woods and across the railway line to the lake, imitating film stars and playing cowboys and Indians, just as they had seen at the cinema.

The familiar shouts of Josh Cogan strained across the meadow as he walked his dog. The boys quickly stamped on their cigarette butts and scarpered through a hole in the rear wall and out into the woods and then to the relative safety of the embankment which carried the railway to their village of Ballynamarbh.

Exhausted after their running, they rested on the sun-warmed grassy embankment.

"I've a stitch." Said Alfie, gasping while nursing a sharp pain at his right ribcage. They stretched out on the warm embankment, wordless and panting for breath after the race through *Sherwood Forest*.

"Wha'da we do now?" Said George.

Pete was staring at the sky. "Home, I s'pose. .... shush .... D'ya hear it?... Iron horse."

They scurried to the top of the embankment and lay flat on their stomachs with their ears against the shiny brown steel track, just like they had seen Indian scouts doing in the westerns.

"Iron Horse .... two miles." Said Pete.

They gazed and listened along the railway tracks which shimmered in the summer heat before vanishing to a soundless point in the hazy distance where a dot grew bigger and bigger. Then chugging and puffing, the iron symphony grew louder and louder as it burst through the lazy, rural peace. A long piercing hoot warned of the train's approach. The boys waited, crouching, on the grassy embankment, like bandits ready to ambush.

Pete looked at Alfie. "Your turn."

Alfie said nothing. He was very aware that Pete knew that he was scared, but scared or not, he would have to go through with it. He had to prove that he was good enough to be with them; one of the gang or so he thought.

Alfie stood poised, readying himself like an athlete waiting for the starting gun and trying desperately to hide the fear that he knew was all over his face. Menacingly, the locomotive advanced nearer, nearer, nearer; its fire and smoke, steam and pistons, metal clanging on metal, all blasting into a deafening, exhilarating crescendo. Alfie made his dash, feeling the breeze as the gigantic locomotive with its massive wheels roared past his back. His momentum brought him to the bottom of the embankment on the other side of the tracks. He turned, looking up at what he had beaten; an army of metal wheels slicing their way unforgivingly along the track. The long train of freight wagons took its brazen time to pass before receding with all its violent commotion away down the line, leaving its sulphurous trail in the air while the summer silence returned.

Alfie lay there in a cold sweat thinking of what he had done and that by now he could have been sliced to pieces with bits of his body strewn along the tracks.

"Ya can get up now, varmint." Said Pete, his toy rifle pointed at Alfie's head. Alfie grinned a smug grin. He had passed a test of manhood.

The railway line stretched in a long, broad curve towards the village of Ballynamarb. The village consisted of a main street off which were a few lanes which led out into the fields. The main street sloped gently down towards a small railway halt and a stone arched railway bridge which cut the village off from the farmland beyond. The Catholic church, St Vincent's, stood, commanding, at the top of the village street. One family, the O'Neills, owned the grocer's shop, along with the hardware shop which seemed to sell anything and everything. A telephone kiosk and a green pillar box stood on the pavement outside the post office. Beside the post office, O'Connor's public house stood welcoming.

Opposite O'Connor's, the Garda station kept a watchful eye on things. *"Cute whores! They can spy on us from over there."* Was how one old regular at the pub would refer to the uncomfortable proximity of the Garda Station. The primary school, a joyless Victorian building with its concreted yard and high railings, stood obediently next to the church.

Four cars, a Ford Consul, an Austin Cambridge, a Hillman Minx and a Ford Anglia, all with their standard coating of beige country mud, could be seen parked regularly on the

Main Street. It could have been siesta time in some Spanish village as the sun baked down on the almost deserted little Irish street.

The clip clop, clip clop of horse hooves echoed through the stone arch bridge beneath the railway line. Garda Phil Keane, barely shaving and in his first year out of training school, remained in his chair which he had leaning back against the wall with his legs stretching towards his desk, the heels of his size tens balancing on the edge. Merely curious, he stretched his upper body to one side, straining his neck to peer through the open window. *Tinkers,* he thought, as he watched the Romany caravan with its weathered green canvass, moving slowly past.

Keane sprang into action, his chair falling upright as he sat forward and he picked up the phone. Sergeant Crilly at a village, a few miles away, answered Keane's call.

"Hello Gerry, Phil Keane here. There's a lone Tinker's caravan just passed by. Do you have any word on it?"

"Not really." Said Crilly. It passed through here a couple of hours ago. Never seen 'em before. Just the one caravan. Looks like a young girl on her own. Probably more of 'em in the back. Ya just wouldn't know with them."

"Strange." Said Keane. "No trouble from her?"

"None at all …. just seemed to be passing through. Stopped for water and a quick bit of the usual begging and she was away down the road."

The barefooted Anna Louise Caddy held the reins near to the bridle, coaxing the old cart horse along the street.

Her flaxen hair lay in unruly tufts on her shoulders. A green summer smock hung loose around her body and her bare legs and arms had a healthy summer tan.

Garda Keane's eyes followed the caravan as it stopped by the water trough. Just a few refreshing gulps were all the horse was allowed in such intense heat and after a morning of pulling his load, just enough to keep him going but not so much as might make him sick. He could drink more, later. Anna Louise bent over the water trough, taking the opportunity to freshen herself, scooping a few handfuls of the cool water onto her face.

The Tinker girl looked around the near deserted street as she led the horse and caravan away from the trough and continued up the slight incline. Deserted the street may well have been but she was well aware that she hadn't gone unnoticed. She could almost feel the curtains twitching as the good citizens of Ballynamarbh spied on her from the comfort and *safety* of their homes.

People always kept an eye on her sort, always made sure that their doors were locked at night and during the day too when the Tinkers were around. Anna Louise had become used to it, used to the mistrust, the taunts, the accusations, and the sheer bloody cruelty of the supposed Christian people …. *Tinkers, knackers, gippos about* …. People would say …. *watch your property, watch your back. Never drink with a Tinker and never let them see your wallet.* Anna Louise knew, of course, that there were a few *daycent people around*, the few who would always give a cup of milk or some old clothes. Yes, there were always a few.

She halted the caravan in a shaded spot near to the Catholic church, unhitched the horse and tethered him to a tree with a long rope and settled him with a clump of sweet-smelling grass. She hauled herself up between the shafts and stepped into the caravan.

"You alright Mam?" She said to her mother who lay propped-up on her bunk. "Is the pain still there?"

Her mother smiled. "Ah, it's not too bad now, love." She fibbed.

The pain in her chest was much worse than it had been earlier that morning, but she didn't want to worry her daughter any more than she had to. Anna Louise poured cool water from a jug into a tin cup and held it to her mother's lips.

"Mam, will ya drink something?"

"Later love, later. Let you go on now. See if the villagers are in a generous mood." Her mother said, pushing the cup away and coughing a long barking cough.

Anna Louise climbed down from the caravan and stood in the shade of the trees on the roadside by the church. Even in the sunshine, St Vincent's church looked solemn and austere beneath its grey slate roof where a couple of crows squawked mournfully from their high perches as if self-appointed harbingers of doom. She looked down along the Main Street. The blue-uniformed Garda was all too plain to see as he stood next to the green phone kiosk, his eyes fixed on the caravan. Not wanting to engage the policeman visually or otherwise, she quickly looked away.

A stone wall with a light coating of moss, stretched beneath the trees to the lych-gate. Anna Louise went to the gate where she stood looking along the gritty path, between the old headstones, towards the church door. She stared, wondering what it would be like inside. Unable to read; the inscriptions on the old headstones were meaningless to her. Many of the headstones were so ancient that they no longer stood upright. A sharp contrast of bright sunlight and dark shadows cut across a row of yew trees. She had never been in a church before, not even to be baptised, not that she even knew what baptism was. *The priest will help me.* She told herself …. *kind people are priests* …. at least they were supposed to be. She paused for another moment in the full shade of one of the tall trees. She was looking at the church door as if a great deliberation was playing in her mind.

The Tinker girl moved forward as if being drawn. She had this sort of thing happen to her before; an inner voice, something that was guiding her. It never bothered her. She thought that everyone had an inner voice. It was only natural. It was something she just took for granted. But she did have a feeling that somehow, she was special and able to see into other worlds.

She stepped through into the porch at the entrance. The old tiles felt smooth beneath her bare feet. Parish notices were pinned to a board. Increasingly these days she found herself wishing she could read. The heavy door swung easily with a slight squeak as it opened into the body of the church. She stepped inside but was startled as the heavy door swung to a clanging, echoing close behind her. She was there now and would see it through.

Shafts of dust speckled sunlight angled through the high stained-glass windows down onto the rows of empty, silent pews. Anna Louise had been in lonely, deserted places before, but she never had quite such a feeling of being so alone as she had right then. It was as if the hills and the woods and the riverbanks were her real home and places such as this, huge, cavernous buildings, where even her cough seemed to bounce about somewhere in the background, were alien to her.

She stood silent at the back of the church, her eyes scanning upwards to the high vaulted ceiling. So very high .... *how did they get up there to paint it?* She wondered. She looked at the tall windows with their brilliant colours, blues and reds and greens like jars of sweets, all lit up by the sun. She wondered about the pictures along the walls, the Stations of the Cross. She had no knowledge of the significance of churches or the story of Christ. The statue of the Virgin Mary occupied a special place by the altar. Small candles glowed beneath the statue. She had seen this same statue many times before at roadside grottos.

Anna Louise looked at the altar. She moved along the aisle and sat in one of the pews. She had never prayed before, but she had seen others doing it at the roadside grottos or when the bells rang for the Angelus at noon and in the evenings. All she knew was that they prayed to God, and he would make everything alright.

"Please make Mam better." She whispered. "Please God, if you are really there, please make her better."

The walls around her remained silent. She felt nothing. "Please God. Make Mam better." She whispered again. She closed her eyes, and then it was as if the building were moving slowly around her. Noises came at first. Noises like the sound of people arguing but they were confused noises, disjointed, incoherent and they disturbed her. She looked around but there was no one there. The noise stopped for a moment then came again, clearer this time, complete words, but she could not understand them, strange sounding words. Were they words from some far away land? She was confused.

The church became silent again; warm, peaceful but Anna Louise had a feeling that she should not be there, that somehow someone or something didn't want her to be there but also, she had the exact opposite feeling that someone or something did want her to be there. Yes, there was something about this place, conflicting forces.

She stood up and as she turned to leave, she came face to face with the priest who had been there for a while, observing her. He was standing in the middle of the aisle, blocking her way. He was a tall thin man wearing a long black frock with a stiff, white, uncomfortable looking collar. A cold stare from his dark piercing eyes put fear into her.

"What are you doing child?" He said with an aggressive tone.

"I was only lookin' Boss, only prayin'." She said, trying to sound pious.

"Well, you've said your prayers. Now off with you." He said, pointing to the door.

Anna Louise stared at him for a moment as a scene flashed through her mind, a scene that she was able to connect with the voices she had heard just a few minutes before. Meekly, she stepped around the priest, walking back along the aisle and out into the sunlight, feeling like some wretched second-class citizen, as anyone would, having had such a reception in the so-called house of God. She stopped for a moment at the lych-gate, looking back at the church, pondering the things she had seen and heard and the unfriendliness of that priest.

The Garda was still there, hovering uneasily about the Main Street as Anna Louise knocked on doors, looking for old clothes and any spare food that the people might have. This was how she and her mother lived their lives, hand to mouth, day to day. Some people would not answer her knock, some people would give a polite, but firm brush off and some would slam the door in her face but there were always a few who were kind.

Her mother was asleep when she returned to the caravan. The sun had moved further along its daily arc, its warm rays now falling on the green canvass. Anna Louise hitched the old carthorse between the shafts and led the caravan away down the Main Street. The caravan moved, as slowly as a funeral cortege, down towards the railway bridge. A few people who were now going about their business or idly gossiping on the street, stopped to see the barefoot Tinker girl with her horse and colourful caravan and it was as if they were looking at something from another world. Anna Louise felt the eyes of the policeman burning into her back as she led the horse and caravan into the shade beneath the bridge.

Carmel Caddy had been thinking quite a bit while she lay on her bunk in the caravan. From her line of sight, through the caravan door, the tops of trees moved slowly against the bright blue sky. She knew her time was near. She wanted to find a place, a peaceful remote place where she could be laid to rest and never be disturbed.

Intuition made Anna Louise stop the caravan about a mile beyond the bridge. She spoke to her mother through the open caravan door.

"I think there's a place along here Mam." She said. "It'll be grand."

Carmel didn't answer, leaving the decision to her daughter. The colourful wagon turned off the road and followed a rutted track which ran through a low, narrow arch beneath the railway embankment. Anna Louise heard something again. It was as if that something was guiding her. She didn't tell her mother about her intuition and the voices in her head.

She had never been to Ballynamarbh before, but she felt a haunting there. It was if she was being called back to another time, another life of which she had been a part.

The roof of Caqueux House was visible in the distance and then the dirt track ended. The way was still clear enough and the old horse pulled his load into a wood. It was quiet there with only the chatter of birds flitting about between the branches. Anna Louise kept going for another while, somehow knowing that it would be evident when she should stop.

There it was. She had found the place she had seen in her mind. She knew instinctively that this was where she was meant to come, a glade in the woods with a carpet of soft grass and with shafts of sunlight squinting between the trees.

Unbuckling the heavy harness, Anna Louise unhitched the cart horse and tied it to a tree with a long stretch of fraying rope. Her first task, as always, was to take care of the horse. A half bucket of water, some feed and as much grass as he could tear from the ground around him. She gathered kindling, expertly building a fire over which she hung a blackened pot with the remainder of a rabbit stew from the previous night. The girl ate her supper from a tin bowl as she sat on the wooden steps of the caravan while her mother stayed in her bunk, taking just a few spoons of the hot stew.

Later, as the sun was going down behind Cogan's farm, mother and daughter were tucked up in their bunks with part of the canvass rolled back so they could see the night sky in comfort. Carmel used these moments to instruct her daughter about life and especially about men, not so much about the physical aspect of men but more about their minds. Anna Louise was thirteen years old and knew nearly all there was to know about sex and men.

"See how the trees look mighty and tall from down here." Said Carmel. "D'ya see how we seem to be only small twigs as we look up at them, how they seem to touch the sky."

Anna Louise said nothing, her eyes focusing on the darkened treetops silhouetted against the deep wondrous inky sky beyond, making her momentarily confused as to whether she was looking up at a great height or down into a great depth.

"But we know that we have power over the giant trees." Said Carmel. "We know that all we have to do is to take an axe and we can cut one down so that it lies dead on the ground. That is how you must see men. Never let 'em get the better of ya. They'll seem bigger and stronger than you but there will always be a way for you to get the better of them."

None of this was new to Anna Louise. Carmel had instilled a deep mistrust of men in her daughter and for good reason too. Anna Louise remembered the many times when, as a frightened child, she hid under the caravan as her father, maddened with the drink, would beat her mother.

The girl pulled the canvass forward, fastening the ties, blocking out the night sky and she put another blanket over her mother's legs and returned to her own warm bunk.

Carmel watched the slight figure of her daughter beneath the patched quilt, justifying to herself that she was right to have taken her little girl away from the family into a life where they would have to fend for themselves. She thought about the last night at the camp when her husband, drunk and violent, fondled his own daughter. After a lifetime of accepting his slaps, kicks, punches, drinking, foul language and humiliation, Carmel found her inner strength when he went for Anna Louise. That was the last straw. She wasn't going to let her own daughter be abused and brutalised. Years of misery welled up inside Carmel. She grabbed hold of a heavy pan and with all her might and willpower she walloped her husband across the head. Other members of the clan watched in awe as the fired-up woman dragged his drunken body from the caravan, dumping it with contempt at their feet. They watch as the raged woman hitched up her horse and drove the caravan out of the camp away into the night, leaving a life of misery to anyone who was stupid or terrified enough to suffer it. Now, even though she was a sick woman, Carmel Caddy felt content and whispered words of thanks to nature for the peace that this place was giving her.

The sun came up over the lake beyond the railway embankment and its morning light scintillated through the trees. Anna Louise rekindled the fire. They ate a breakfast of boiled eggs with bread and tea. After breakfast Carmel felt strong enough to walk around the glade. "Must keep my strength up," she thought. They wouldn't have to travel for a while, now that they had found this nice, isolated place where no one would bother them.

Anna Louise washed her and her mother's clothes, a laborious, physical task but it was good weather for drying. She pegged the wet clothes along a rope which she had stretched between two trees where the warmth of the mid-morning sun was strong. Carmel spent much of the day making charms in her sickbed.

Her chores completed; Anna Louise set about making herself pretty. She spent a while in front of her mirror, combing her flaxen hair. She pouted, practising vulnerability, using her deep blue eyes to mesmerise. She stood back to see her entire body. She slinked her hands along her curves and around her bottom, making a half turn to see her back. She was thinking of what it would be like to be with a man, how it would feel to be so close to another person, how he would react to her and how she would react to him and what it would feel like when she teased a man. A satisfied smile came to her face as she thought of the wanting stares of men, of their lingering lustful looks and she knew that there was something special about her own self.

Her girlish fantasies were interrupted by the distant shouts of children at play. Curious; Anna Louise crept stealthily towards the commotion, taking cover from tree to tree and then more loud hollers .... nearer now. She moved forward, crouching in the undergrowth. She could see them now. Three boys of about her own age, perhaps a little younger, were running in circles around the trees. She spied from her vantage place as they played with their flimsy, boy-made bows and arrows. After a while they ran off and she followed them as they headed towards the old farm ruins, their *Alamo.* Barefooted, the Tinker girl moved furtively along the edge of the meadow beneath a canopy of hawthorns.

At the *Alamo,* Pete and Alfie and George were playing at fencing with swords made with the wood of old orange boxes. George had fenced Pete across the dirt floor and had him stuck in a corner. Alfie joined in the rout and between them, they had Pete on the defensive, for once.

"Two against one. It's not fair." Pete moaned as they held the toy swords to his throat. "Look! Someone's watching us."

"Nice try." Said George, smiling.

"No honest." Said Pete. "There's girl there, a Tinker."

Alfie and George looked around, but there was no one there. "Liar, liar." They both exclaimed at the same time. Pete pushed past them, rushing to look outside the walls of the *Alamo.* They ran after him, following him around the outside of the old ruin.

"Only rats 'n' dirty varmints out there." Said George.

"I swear. There really was a Tinker girl there." Said Pete, seeing the dubious faces of his pals. "Cross my heart and hope to die …. Swear to God."

They filed back towards the front of the *Alamo,* Pete leading as usual and as he turned to go through the opening in the wall, he stopped dead in his tracks and with that his friends shunted into him, like a three-car pile-up.

The Tinker girl was standing in the middle of the dirt floor. Part girl, part woman, her brushed flaxen hair, looked silky in the sunlight. The boys, now standing abreast, stared in silence as a gentle breeze made her dress cling to her body. Her bare feet seemed to blend into the dry, weedy earth. Her eyes stared, penetrating with a bewitching countenance.

"You a Tinker?" Pete blurted out

She didn't answer.

"I said …. are you a Tinker?"

"What if I am?" Said Anna Louise, defiantly.

"What d'ya want, Tinker?"

"Nothing."

"Well, this is our hideout. No girls and no Tinkers."

"Yeh." Said George, emboldened by Pete's arrogance.

Alfie didn't say anything. He just looked meek and felt uneasy about being party to this unkindness to another person.

"Buy a lucky charm?" She said, jangling her bracelets at them.

Pete shook his head.

"It's unlucky not to buy from a Tinker. Beware the Blue Moon."

"Don't care." Said Pete, crossing his fingers, behind his back.

More silence …… more staring ……

"Tell you what." Said Pete. "You wanna play with us then show us those." He raised his arm, pointing at the girl's breasts.

George smiled mischievously and Alfie blushed.

Anna Louise was amused but didn't show it.

"Mmm." Just who do ya tink ya are?" She said.

"Bad Jake from yonder mountain." Said Pete.

The boys burst into laughter.

"So how 'bout it Honey?" He said with his mock cowboy accent.

Anna Louise stared at the boys for a moment, making them feel uneasy that they crossed some moral line. But she nodded her head.

"Thruppence each then, and that's for a feel only not a look."

The boys couldn't believe it. Pete's brazenness had paid off. He dug into his pockets.

"Yeh. I have three pence." Said Pete.

George also produced a thruppenny bit.

Alfie fumbled about for a while and eventually found two penny coins. With his dirty fingernails, he held them up triumphantly. Anna Louise shrugged. Tuppence for you then.

Pete moved forward but she pushed her hand out to stop him.

"Hold on. I'll be in there." She said, pointing towards another room of the old building. "Wait 'till I call ya. One at a time."

She twirled about feeling the stares of their curious eyes. She went through an opening into what had once been another room. A few dusty timber planks made for somewhere to sit. Her mother's voice came into her head. *"Always make 'em wait. Always make 'em pay. Always let them enjoy it more than you do. Then they will always want more, and you will always have more. Be calm inside and never let them see that you enjoy it."*

The wait, only a minute or two, seemed like ages to the boys. For each of them, this was to be their first physical encounter with a girl. One minute they were playing as children and the next they were going to feel a girl's breasts for the very first time. They didn't really know what they were doing; boys on the cusp between childhood and adolescence, just messing about, trying to act big. They had been taught that it was a sin to talk about the private parts of the human body and especially they were not to talk about girls' private parts. This forbidden fruit made it all the more exciting to them. They loved to say words like bum, fanny, tits, prick but had not yet been told about sex except that which they picked up from the older children in the school yard. They each had had secret crushes on girls but had no idea why or what it was all about. All they knew was that one or two girls in their community were in some way special to them. They liked being near them or with them and wanted to touch them. But in their puerile world, girls were different. Girls had their own ways, and they were different from boys.

"Ya ever felt tits before?" Said Pete.

George shook his head and poor little Alfie just felt sick.

"Ya can't squeeze 'em too hard or ya'll get milk." Said George, trying to sound as if he knew things.

"Naw. That's only when they are married and have babies." Said Pete.

"Is it?"

Pete shrugged. "Yeh and if ya drink a Tinker's milk then ya can turn into the devil."

The soft girlish voice floated through the air. "Who's first."

Pete looked at George. "You first." He said.

"No. It was your idea."

"Ok." Pete said, as he stepped across the dirt floor and into the lair.

Anna Louise remained seated. She pouted as if she had done this a thousand times before, but this was her very first encounter too. Pete had his head slightly bowed, his eyes on her chest. She scrutinised his face, learning the expressions of a boy, trying to read his thoughts. Clumsily, he groped her breasts through her dress. She had already formed an opinion of this boy. The thought went through her mind that he might grow up to be a right bastard. He was there to get whatever he could for his own pleasure and a woman would find it very hard to control him.

"That's your thruppence worth." She said as if she had measured it all out.

Pete looked as if he had been cheated. His hand groped for more.

"Enough." She said, her voice commanding.

Pete backed away, somehow aware that unwritten laws were now in force. He went back into where his pals were waiting nervously and gave the thumbs up sign with a big grin on his face,

"Next." She called out, business-like.

George stood in the opening that had once been a door. Anna Louise looked at him. He hesitated before taking a few steps forward and hesitated again.

"Well, don't ya want your money's worth?"

"I want a kiss as well." Said George.

She took his hand and placed it on her right breast. He could feel her nipple through her clothes. Her eyes closed as she pushed her chin into the air, inviting him to kiss her on the neck. George smooched his lips just below her right earlobe. She had a sort of earthy sweet smell. His heart quickened as he felt a trembling sensation all over his body and inexplicable sensations in his lower stomach and groin area which made him want to press against her body. Anna Louise could sense the power that she had over him at that moment. She could feel his want, his all-consuming need but also his immature confusion. She knew that he would do whatever she wanted. She pushed her chin further into the air as George's eager, wanting mouth followed. She was tempted to succumb to his gentleness but remembered her mother's words. Her lips remained closed as his lips met hers. He kissed them once and moved back. It was all over in less than a minute but to George it seemed like a kind of forever and maybe it was.

Alfie sat nervously against a wall.

"Your turn." Said George who was feeling somewhat stunned.

"Go on." What are ya waiting for?" Said Pete.

Alfie had a bewildered look on his face. Pete pushed him, making him stumble into where the Tinker girl was waiting. The least mature and most insecure of the three boys didn't want to do this at all, but he didn't want to be seen to funk out, especially now that the others had gone through with it. Clumsily, he stumbled forward, reaching out, awkwardly touching the girl's breast. He quickly took his hand away being at once struck with the thought that he had just committed a sin, and a mortal sin at that, and now he was going to have to include it on his list of sins for confession to the priest.

Alfie was gone, leaving the Tinker girl to ponder her encounter with the boys. She felt good about the fact that men, even though they were only boys, wanted to pay her money for the pleasure of her body. She had learned from them, how men could be so different; one shy and backward, she didn't want this type. Neither did she want the type like the first boy, who might turn out to be a cold-hearted brute. No, she thought, the second boy would be her type; daring but gentle; strong but not as strong as she herself was. He would be the type that she could manipulate while at the same time he would be good enough to make her happy and if it all ended then, surely, she would not be the one to cry. However, she had made one mistake.

Anna Louise swept her hands through her thick hair as she went back to where the boys were.

"I'll have my money now." She said, her bejewelled arm stretched out for payment.

Pete laughed with contempt. Alfie and George let out a supporting snigger. She knew she had made a mistake, a mistake she would remember, but she wasn't about to lose face.

"Are you going to pay me for what you have taken? For what you owe me!

The boys laughed again.

"For what?" A feel of those. You must be joking. I've felt bigger blackberries." Said Pete, remembering something he heard some older boys once say.

Maddened and furious inside, Anna Louise's countenance changed to that of a scorned woman. She stared at each of them in turn.

"You owe me thruppence. You owe me thruppence and you owe me a tuppence. Now do I get it or else?"

"Or else what?" Said Pete. "You'll put a curse on us?"

"Yeh." She said, with anger in her voice. "I will curse you. Be warned."

Too scared to say anything; Alfie crossed himself. George really wanted to pay but said nothing. Pete forced a defiant laugh.

"Come on guys. Let's vamoose." Said Pete.

Anna Louise remained alone among the ruins for a while. Thoughts of her old life on the road with her extended family came to her mind. Back then she could only watch helpless when the brutality raged. But this was different. Now, she liked the sense of her own controlled rage. It felt natural that she should demand payment in some form for the needs of others, even if it was only a puerile game. But they hadn't paid. They had made a fool of her, used her, taken advantage, stolen from her. She would get what she had earned and make them pay, one way or another, not only for what they had taken but more especially for making a fool of her.

She stood looking at the crumbling walls, sensing the presence of those who had been there before, away back in the mists of time. Images ghosted in the air, fleeting spectral images, ghosts of people from the past. There surely had been at least one horrific and tragic occurrence there. It was all around her now. She could smell it, death, fear, anger, terror and the sense of an urgent pressing need for revenge. But she wasn't afraid. She had been reared with the belief that all things, the woods, the hedgerows, the mountains, the lakes, the rivers, the oceans, the skies and the heavens beyond were all one and that evil was just another part of the deal. She could use evil to her own advantage. The past sent her the sound of a baby crying and an image of an old woman lying helpless on the ground. Then she saw something that would have frozen the blood of most people. An image of a girl of about her own age stared out from the mists of time. The girl seemed to be reaching out to Anna Louise. The girl's belly had been ripped open. She was screaming, pleading for help, desperate for deliverance. The evil was engulfed in a fireball and in an instant it vanished.

The *Alamo* was again its quiet benign self. Anna Louise could feel her heart thumping in her chest with the consternation of what she had just seen, but she fixed her mind to cope with it, returning her thoughts to the boys.

Thinking about her first encounter with boys, Anna Louise felt pleased by the fact that she liked being touched in that way. It gave her a feeling of elation that she never had experienced before. She was thinking about the second boy as she walked beneath the shady canopy of overhanging hawthorn trees. She remembered the almost overpowering sensations in her body as his gentle kisses brushed the soft skin of her neck as she pushed her chin higher with each wanting kiss. She leaned against a tree, imagining that he was there, their bodies hard against each other. It felt good, thinking about him with his adoring kisses. Realising her anger again, she bounced those pleasure thoughts away. He would still have to pay, pay a debt of honour because he was a man and a debt of nature for what she considered to be the proper order of things. She would not tell her mother about her encounter with the boys.

The golden meadow shimmered lazily in the hot afternoon sun. Wildflowers splashed the countryside with vivid rainbow colours. Anna Louise looked towards Josh Cogan's house. Like a prowling cat, she fused with the hedgerows, flitting towards the white-washed walls of the farmyard. Like a fox, she peered cautiously through the gate. A few chickens strutted moronically on the lazy warm cobble stones, while a snoozy black Labrador languished in the shade by an open door. She knew that the dog would just lie there, happily dozing. Animals never bothered her. It was as if she and they had some mutual understanding, kindred spirits. She climbed over the gate and into the yard. An old hen wandered close to her and suddenly she had it by the neck. The old dog didn't even blink, the hen never knew what hit it and Anna Louise had her supper.

Old Meg had been watching and was waiting for the Tinker girl to climb back over the gate. Anna Louise froze, the chicken still protesting in her grip as she came face to face with the wizened old housemaid. They stared at each other as if fate or destiny were somehow binding them. Neither of them knew what it was or might be but they both felt something, something supernatural. Old Meg turned and walked away as if she had seen nothing, nothing at all.

When she returned to the caravan, Anna Louise plucked the bird, preparing it for the pot, keeping some of the best feathers, the feet and the head which she hung on a tree near the caravan. When it was ready, she put the stolen fowl into a blackened pot of simmering water, along with vegetables and herbs. She fixed the pot on a metal tripod over the fire.

Carmel felt well enough to leave her bunk and together they ate their supper by the campfire with the setting sun's flame-red rays squinting low through the trees. After supper,

Carmel went back to her bunk while her daughter washed the bowls and put away any uneaten food. Then Anna Louise sat on the ground within the warmth of the fire and tucked her knees beneath her chin with her arms wrapped around her folded legs. She was reflecting the day's events. Stealing a chicken from a rich farmer was nothing to her. She had done that many times before, as well as eggs from hen houses, apples from orchards, potatoes from the fields, bread from unattended bakers' vans, cool fresh milk from shining steel churns or anything that would fill her belly and keep her alive for another while. She had stolen money too but that was mostly from the pockets of wealthy racegoers at point-to-point meetings. .... *Well, they were only going to lose it to the bookies anyway....*

Now, she knew that there was an easier way to make a living, even with her failure to get paid for her first job. Anna Louise knew that she was onto something, something that might help her to survive this harsh world. As the bright flames flickered, enhancing the darkness in the background, she thought about the second boy and in her mind, she projected forward to the days when men would fall over themselves simply to be with her. Tomorrow she would have to settle the score but not before giving those boys one more chance to pay their debt.

Her eyes fixed on the flames which radiated a warm cocoon of orange light in the blackness of the night and high overhead the stars twinkled through the leafy treetops.

The voice came again, whispering through the glade. Anna Louise was still, a willing audience to whatever or whoever it was. As she listened, a strange force seemed to engulf her, and it was as if she had stepped over some invisible threshold.

Wisps of steamy vapour rose from the caravan as the morning sun warmed the damp canvass. Carmel was feeling well enough to leave her bunk and take a stroll through the woods.

"Are you sure you'll be alright, now Mam?" Said Anna Louise.

"I'll be grand, love. If I've not many days like this left in me then I surely will make the most of them. Anyways, a lovely day in a beautiful place is always good for the spirit and so it is good for the body. Besides, I must have a talk with those who came before us."

Alone, Anna Louise took a small casket from a hiding place beneath her bunk. She placed the casket on her bunk, opening it, as she always did, with a delight and expectation as if she had just found it and was exploring the contents for the very first time. Her slender fingers slipped through the trinkets and the gleaming pieces of jewellery, spooning them over the open casket. Her eyes sparkled brighter than the jewels as she gazed on them with a feminine avarice before letting them cascade through her fingers and back into the treasure casket.

Scrooge-like, her fingers picked through her treasures, selecting rings. One ring was special, depicting two moons.

She rubbed it against her frock, enhancing its shine. It had been handed down through the generations of her family's women and for the past four years Anna Louise Caddy had been its keeper. As she slipped it onto her right little finger with a girlish flourish, she remembered the day when she was ten years old and was sent by her mother to the caravan of old Nan O'Reilly. Nan, the matriarch of the family, was on her deathbed. Anna Louise was to be the last person to see Nan alive. That was a family tradition. She remembered how she dreaded the very thought of going into that old woman's caravan and going in alone too. Reluctantly, but dutifully, she climbed the steps of old Nan's caravan and entered, giving the respect that a dying family elder was due.

The smell of death was there, pungent in the air around old Nan. She looked so frail with her leathery face sunk into the pillow and her nothing body making little impression beneath the patchwork blanket that was to be her last earthly comfort. Her grey hair lay in scrawny pigtails on her chest and her still twinkling eyes rolled in reddened sockets as she looked at the young unblemished bright face.

Even now, Anna Louise could still feel the old woman's claw-like grip as she took her by the wrist. Her voice was feeble but clear in its determination.

"You are young but still have duties." Said Nan. "Take the ring from my finger."

Anna Louise remembered looking at the slender, knotty fingers.

"Go on, take it." Said Nan.

Shy and wordless, the little girl did as she was told and slipped the ring with the two moons from old Nan's right little finger onto her own right little finger. It was loose on the smaller younger digit.

"Keep it safe until it fits. With this ring you will possess great powers of womanly wisdom." Said Nan, her voice was weak and strained.

Anna Louise sat on the edge of the dying woman's bunk. She wasn't afraid now, feeling some strange inner comfort. Even at such a young age, she somehow knew that this was all part of the time-honoured rites of her family. All of this was special. It was duty.

"You know what you have to do now?" Nan whispered.

Anna Louise nodded.

"You are not afraid?"

Anna Louise shook her head. "No. I will stay with you."

The soft light from an oil lamp made shadows flicker about the caravan as she began the death vigil. She sat beside the matriarch all through the long night and just as the sun came up again, old Nan coughed and rattled in her throat and died. Anna Louise laid the leathery hands across Nan's chest and kissed her forehead.

The other women had been keeping vigil outside all through the long night. Anna Louise felt a twinge of nervous importance as she announced to the small gathering that Mamma Nan had crossed over to the other side and that her earthly wisdom and powers had been passed on. She held the Moon ring aloft for everyone to see. Now, she was remembering how special that night had been, how important she felt in the scheme of things. It was special.

Her thoughts returned to the present. Anna Louise fixed her mirror so that she could see as much of herself as was possible. She posed, admiring herself with her adornment of rings and bracelets and earrings. Not enough! She thought, wanting to be as bewitching as possible. More colours, more things that glistened, more things that would attract attention, female weaponry, Romany female weaponry. She tied a bright red ribbon to her hair and puckered her lips as she looked in the mirror, then she reached for a more dazzling pair of earrings.

When she was ready, Anna Louise Caddy did indeed feel like a grown-up woman. She would easily have passed as an eighteen-year-old. She practiced her posing, looking vulnerable one minute and then in an instant changing her countenance to that of a cold calculating bitch.

Closing the caravan door, she fixed a sprig of lilac over it and cursed anyone who tried to enter without an invitation. She went along the dirt track towards the *Alamo,* willing the three boys to be there but as she approached the *Alamo,* she could not hear any playful shouts.

The crumbling old place was silent, but the boys were there all right. Barefoot and blending with the ivy and moss clad, perished masonry, she crept forward and then she was still, listening as the boys talked quietly behind one of the old walls.

"D'ya think the Tinker's curse was real?" She heard one of them say.

"Naw." Said another. "They all say things like that …. She was only bluffing."

"Nice tits though." Said another, trying to act big.

They stopped talking as she appeared in the opening in the wall. She looked different to how she had appeared the day before. Her eyes were fixed on the dirt floor, her head bent slightly forward as if at their mercy. No one said anything for a few long seconds. Then slowly she raised her head and her countenance seemed to change. The big blue eyes had turned to a steely grey. She seemed taller now.

"Oh! but it is a real curse …. I have special powers."

Pete laughed and George forced a back-up chuckle, but poor little Alfie looked scared to death.

"Are you going to pay what you owe me?"

The boys didn't answer. Poker-faced, she waited for a moment. Then with an outstretched arm she pointed her accusing witchy finger at each of them in turn.

"Then you are all damned. With this Moon ring, I damn each of you. Beware the Blue Moon." Her words raged in their ears.

With a determined contempt, she spat three times and with a delicate and resolute action of her stretched right foot, she ground each spit into the brown earth. She stepped backwards to the opening between the walls, all the while keeping an icy stare on her victims. She turned and then it was as if she just disappeared.

Pete ran to the opening to shout abuse at her, but she seemed to have disappeared.

"Where did she go?" His voice was panicky. He turned to his pals.

"Ok then, we'll just put a curse on her."

He danced around his pals, hollering like the Indians he had seen in the westerns, slapping his hand against his open rounded mouth. "Hia, hia, ho .... Hia, hia, ho .... Hia, hia, ho." George and Alfie joined in, following Pete in circles through the clumps of weed and the fallen masonry. Louder and louder, they chanted. "Wow, wow, wow, wow, hia, hia ho, wow, wow, wow."

They chased about for several minutes. Pete spat on the dirt, rubbing his fingers in it to make war-paint which he smeared across his face. He continued with the dance, now accompanying it with a monk-like chant. "Begone curse of the Tinker .... wooo .... Begone curse, begone, begone, begone. Hia, hia, ho .... Hia, hia, ho .... Wow, wow, wow, wow ...." George and Alfie imitated Pete, following him around the old *Alamo* ruins as if they were in a frenzy. Then they collapsed on the ground in fits of laughter.

"D'ya think she can really put a curse on us?" Said Alfie.

"What can Tinkers do?" Said George. "Sure, they can't even read."

"We could get a disease from touching her." Said Pete. "We might even grow tits ourselves."

At once they all felt their own chests. Pete reached to Alfie's chest, rubbing it.

"Yeh, you definitely have a tit growing there." He laughed.

"Haven't, have I?" Said Alfie, taking the bait and looking worried.

"Stupid." Said George as Alfie stood up; tucking his chin back so he could peer down at his chest.

Anna Louise kept affirming the curse as she walked back to the glade. The more she thought about the boys, the more she willed evil on them. The only weakness in her spell was that she liked George, 'the second boy'. But then she thought of her mother's words about being soft on a man, any man. "Never show any softness. Let 'em think you are soft but never be soft."

The sun was very bright, making her shade her eyes with her hand to look across towards Cogan's farm. She wondered what it would be like to live in a house. *Could never sleep under a roof.* She told herself …. *always being in the same place …. walls! …. couldn't breathe!* She shuddered at the very thought. No, the life of ever-changing scenery on the open road beneath the open sky was the only one for her.

She slipped between the trees into the woods. Her mind was worrying now, something she could not name or something she was trying to hide from herself. But she couldn't hide her intuition for long and as she went into the glade, her worst fears were realised.

She wasn't at all surprised to find her mother; collapsed on the ground and gasping for breath.

"Mam, Mam. Oh Mam. You're sick again. I told you not to go too far. Come on, I'll help you into your bed."

Carmel was weak but was still conscious. "No love. The hour is here. I .... I feel it. Let me pass away here." Her voice was weak as she stumbled through her breathless utterances.

Anna Louise hurried into the caravan, grabbed a pillow and a blanket then hurried back to her mother.

"Here Mam." She said, as she lifted her mother's head to make room for the pillow. She tucked the blanket around the thin body and under the feet.

Carmel spoke again.

"You know," she said, "I couldn't have picked a better place to take my last breath."

Anna Louise's eyes glistened as the inevitable tears formed. "I feel so helpless, so useless, Mam. Will ya not let me get help?"

Carmel shook her head. "No love, sure no one can help me now. Let me go here. Have ya looked around? There's something about this place. I know you feel it too."

She coughed again, a rough, barking cough from deep in her chest that wrenched her whole body and it seemed to go on for a long while. She could see the distress on her daughter's face.

"I came into this world with nothing at all, probably born somewhere like this. No one marked my name in any book and only our own folk know that I ever lived. Put me into the ground here and move on." She gripped her daughter's arm. "I want you to promise me .... when I die .... I want you to start digging over there .... do the job right away .... lay me in the ground here .... I know you will do it with love .... then leave this place .... find yourself a man, a wealthy man .... your face will be your fortune .... make the best of it, love." Carmel's voice was soft now. She wanted to say more but knew that love would bind them forever. She closed her eyes and her grip on her daughter's arm loosened and then she was gone. Anna Louise crouched over her dead mother's body, cradling her head in her arms and she stayed that way, rocking gently for a long while.

The sun was at its highest, beaming intensely down through the treetops. Anna Louise wiped away her tears. She took her mother's only frock from the caravan, pulled and stretched it over the lifeless limbs and laid her Mam's body out on the grass. She gathered wildflowers and arranged them carefully on the pillow, pausing from time to time to look at her dear Mam's face. The face was pale now, cold but somehow looked younger as if all the anger and bitterness and the hurt of a hard life had also died, leaving a deathly beauty that maybe only some old Celtic poet could describe.

Satisfied that she had arranged her mother's body with love and respect, Anna Louise took a long-handled shovel from beneath the caravan and selected a place in the glade, not far from where her mother's body lay. Yes, this will be just grand, she told herself. The setting sun will fall right here during the fine summer evenings, like it did the night before, her mother's last night in this life.

"Will this be alright, Mam?" She said, almost aloud as if her mother could still hear her.

She marked out the length and breadth of the plot with the shovel and then she began to dig. The brown earth sliced easily at first, the top clumps coming away with little effort. It wasn't until she had broken the surface that she realised just how hard a job this was going to be. She once watched a man digging a grave, in some village. She remembered how he first marked out the plot, how his huge hands and thick, nicotine-stained fingers gripped the spade and how he swung the pickaxe. Yes, that's what she needed now, a pickaxe, but she would have to make-do without one.

Anna Louise spent the afternoon digging, her small figure gradually disappearing as the rectangular hole became deeper and the mound of earth beside it grew bigger and higher. Digging her own mother's grave; how odd, she thought. Perhaps her senses had been numbed. She kept on breaking the earth as if activity, even such a morbid and exhausting one, was keeping her mind occupied. The shovel slipped clumsily as it hit against stones and the frustrating network of tree roots which were like tentacles spreading out below the ground as much as the branches reached out into the air, high above her head.

It was well into the evening when she stopped digging. The grave was a good deal deeper than Anna Louise was tall, but it was deep enough, she reckoned. The mound of fresh brown earth fanned out beside it. She climbed out, using the rope she had already tied to a tree for hoisting the earth away in a bucket. It was *too late to be burying anyone now*, she thought. Besides, she really wanted to delay the awful task for as long as she could. She wanted to keep her Mam with her forever, but she knew that that was not possible. She would have to go through with it. *Tomorrow*, she thought. *Wait 'till the morning. Bury her in the sunshine with all the birds singing, the way Mam herself would have wanted it.*

The dry twigs and leaves were easy to light and the fire beneath the blackened kettle soon took hold. She sat beside the body of her dead mother, sipping hot tea with her earth-stained hands and mud-smeared face as the night closed in around her. Glaring into the flames, she talked as if Carmel were still alive.

"This is it Mam. I know you told me that it was going to happen .... but I never thought it would be so soon. You've been a good mother, Mam. What'll I do without ya?" Her thoughts were deep, her eyes fixed on the bright warm flames. A haunting Traveller funeral song seeped from her heart, and she sang as she pulled the blanket around her shoulders and lay on the ground beside her mother's body, just like they had so often done before .... just talking, giggling.

The arduous work had exhausted her, and she fell asleep with aching limbs, in the glow of the fire. It was a quiet gentle slumber at first which led to a deeper more profound sleep, unlocking her subconscious mind, her other self and not only the consciousness of her own lifetime but that of other lifetimes, other ages; a consciousness that had been passed down through the generations and perhaps even through the very ether of the universe itself.

Visions came from the dark recesses of her mind. Her mother appeared, walking by her side, along a forest path. They were laughing, sharing life, feeling the warm sun on their backs. The dream turned and suddenly Carmel was a stranger to her. Anna Louise saw herself watching as this strange woman walked off into the sunlight while all around her it grew cold, and the light began to fade.

She could see herself walking along a different path now, leading deeper and deeper into the shadows. Pale gaunt faces peered from behind trees and then she saw a glimmer of light somewhere in the distance. She could see herself heading towards the light, homing in on it, as if it were beckoning her, calling her, enticing her away from the cold and the dark. The light grew brighter. She was warm again and then she paused, seeing that the light was coming from a huge fire. She kept going forward, content that her destiny was somehow linked with the fire. Here was where she was meant to be. Here was her life, her real purpose in creation.

She stood by the fire, the intense heat making little impression on her. Rather, it felt good. A man stood with his back to her, a pitchfork in his hand. She waited, submissive, servant-like, for him to finish whatever it was he was doing at the fire. He turned to her and grinned, an ugly damning grin with raging red eyes, steaming nostrils and from either side of his forehead, stumps of horns protruded. But through all of this, Anna Louise slept a deep sleep.

When Anna Louise woke, the sun was well above the trees, its warm rays glimmering through the leaves and the branches before settling gently on her face. She looked at the still body of her mother, admitting to herself that she really was dead, gone forever, never to return. Must get on with it then, she told herself, knowing that a burial would save the once proud, the once so beautiful woman from the indignity of having anyone witness the rotting of her dead flesh. But first things first …. *must make myself proper, wash, clean up and dress as a respectful mourner should.*

* * *

"Ah go on. Give us a look." Said George.

Pete passed the binoculars to George who took a while to focus.

"Wow." Said George. "Look at that."

"Come on. Give us a look too." Said an impatient Alfie, but George kept a hold of the binoculars.

From their vantage point, crouched on the railway embankment, the binoculars gave them an unobstructed view of the naked Tinker girl as she washed in the lake.

Anna Louise thought she was alone, not that nudity had ever bothered her. Unaware of her puerile audience, she squatted in the shallows, her blistered hands scooping the cool water over her nubile but now sore body.

The boys fought over the binoculars, excited with their naked female find. They watched as she came out of the lake, like some Hollywood diva, and dried herself with a towel beneath the morning sun.

"A real naked broad." Said Pete, letting out a wolf whistle, just like in the films.

Alfie's heart pounded as he looked through the binoculars. "Holy cow." Was all he could say. "Holy cow."

Anna Louise pulled her frock over her head. It settled loosely on her shoulders and around her body, then she made her way back up the embankment, across the railway line and into the woods towards the glade where she would bury her mother's remains.

"This is it." She said, looking at her dead mother's face. "I can't put if off any longer, Mam."

She slipped into a red and yellow frock which she had been given by some kindly woman in a village, weeks before. She arranged some flowers in her hair. And then …. and then it was time.

She spread a blanket on the ground beside her mother's body. The blanket was just the right size for the body, which was stiff now, rigid, lifeless. Just a shell. She tried not to think about it as she strained to drag the deadweight, as respectfully as she could, onto the blanket. She was singing or rather chanting a Tinker's chant as she stitched the blanket together. The skin on her mother's face was cold as she ran her fingers lightly over it. Her mother's face … a part of her forever. Anna Louise leaned over and kissed her mother for the last time. Then she stitched the blanket together there too.

When she was satisfied that she had done as good a job as she could have, Anna Louise dragged the body to the grave. She gazed down into the drying brown earth and even though she had dug it herself and was familiar with every part, it still looked gruesome and permanent. She heaved the shrouded body into the ground, being so very careful not to let it fall and she laid her mother's body to rest as gently as she could.

A handful of wildflowers and a haunting chant were all the ceremony she could give. She gazed down into the grave for a while, wishing the moment to remain forever. She did not want time to move forward. She did not want to shovel the earth onto her mother's body. She did not want to fill that hole which now held her only friend in all the world. She consoled herself with the thoughts of how they had shared their lives and their thoughts and their hopes and their love and now there were no regrets, no regrets at all, only sadness.

The Tinker girl's final act of love for her mother was to lay Carmel's quilt over her shrouded body as it lay in the open grave. Then, ever so gently, slowly and with a sad reluctance, Anna Louise Caddy began the lonely task of shovelling the earth back into the grave and her mother's burial would be complete.

* * *

Alfie noticed a piece of sack cloth entwined with the stones on the railway embankment where they were playing that morning. He tugged at the piece of sack, pulling some stones away with his hands. Eventually the sack cloth came free and with it, a raggedy package. Discarding the outer sack cloth, the inner package was also of sacking, tied up with twine. Pete snatched the package from Alfie and began to unwrap it further as George and Alfie watched with an eager curiosity. With the sack cloth discarded, there remained a wooden cigar box. Pete held the box before him with mischief in his eyes.

"Might be a bomb." He said.

"Or a thousand bucks." Said George.

"Might be a stolen thousand bucks." Said Alfie.

They laughed as Pete prised the lid off with his penknife. Their jaws dropped as the secret within the box was revealed. It was a gun, a pistol or handgun of some sort. George grabbed it.

"Come on, you guys." He shouted, waving the gun about. They ran down the embankment towards the woods like a wild west posse following the baddies.

* * *

Dark stormy clouds loomed menacingly over Ballynamarbh and the surrounding countryside. The electrified air roared menacingly as claps of thunder ripped low over the land. A flock of birds; their formation confused, sought refuge somewhere near the sulking waters of the lake. Lightning flashes scintillated for brief seconds between monstrous leaden hulks of dark cloud that blotted-out the sunlight. Tearing, ripping, cracking noises tore through the woods as mighty trees succumbed to nature, falling helpless to the ground. The rain spat for a short while as if taunting, threatening and then suddenly the flood gates opened, and then it poured out of the heavens.

Ballynamarbh was at the centre of the deluge. Drains were soon overwhelmed, sending torrents of water flooding down towards the railway bridge. Crops bowed under the weight of the sudden deluge and milk curdled in dairy churns. Farms and homes in the district were suddenly without electricity and household pets, farm animals and wild animals alike, cowered as the violent storm wallowed in its loud display of power and destruction.

It was as if something had happened to the area, something had been prodded, spooked, disturbed and had come alive, like some angry monster that had been woken from a deep sleep.

Suddenly, the rain stopped. The countryside was quiet again. A fluorescent blur seemed to glow from the land itself. Then it came, low at first, loudening steadily to a shrieking noise like a siren or perhaps it was a banshee, wailing death out over the land.

A sulphurous light seemed to engulf Caqueux House, particularly in the north facing kitchen where Meg Butler had spent the afternoon cleaning and cooking for Josh Cogan. The storm didn't bother her much. Most Irish country people in those days would have crossed themselves with almost every clap of thunder, sprinkling holy water throughout their home, but not in Caqueux House. Both Meg and her employer, Josh, had long since given up on their religious burdens. A picture of the Sacred Heart did still hang on the kitchen wall, a relic of the days when Josh's parents were alive. He never had the heart to take it down. Besides, it never really bothered him.

Old Meg always felt that little bit more secure when the clouds darkened the sky and when the rain poured. To her it was as if everyone else would also have to hunker down and cocoon themselves from the world, just as she herself lived every single day of her life, whatever the weather. Even in the height of summer she would go around in an old grey-green overcoat and hat. Sickly thick beige stockings permanently encased her legs and black lace-up brogues put the finishing touches to her self-imposed drabness.

Children were afraid of old Meg, and they would hide whenever they saw her coming. From the cover of bushes, older children would watch whenever she passed by on the roadside. They would snigger as they listened to her talking to herself, locked in a world of her own. When she would pass by, they would jump out from their hiding places, calling out cruel names before running off. But she never seemed to take any notice, continuing on her way, as if oblivious to a world which had already done its worst to her. Parents would warn their children to *keep well away* from old Meg, the consensus being that she was dangerous, a loner, the local loony. Few, if any, ever stopped to think that Meg Butler had a heart and a soul and feelings, just like everyone else.

* * *

It was an evening some days after the big storm and as usual Meg sat down to supper with her employer, Josh Cogan. Few words passed between them as they ate under the gaze of the Sacred Heart picture.

Satisfied after his meal, Josh retired, as he always did, to the parlour, for a smoke and to read or to listen to the wireless while Meg cleared-up after their meal. Afterwards she would poke her head around the parlour door to say goodnight, leaving Josh to his pipe, his newspaper and his wireless and his thoughts.

Ever since she had come to work at Caqueux House, Josh had never set foot in the semi basement which came to be Meg's private world where she could be left alone with her books and her memories.

Meg took off her brogues and lay on the bed. She read, again, the letter that she had received that morning. She read it once more before letting it fall from her hand. It floated sideways in the air for a moment before settling on the floor near to the bed. Her eyes fixed on the lifeless official document as it lay on the floor, taking her thoughts back to when she was a child.

Meg's first memories were of being in a large room with a high ceiling from which bare light bulbs hung on long cords. There were other children there too, sleeping in two long rows of cots, an assembly line of small children, all beginning their lives with a huge deficiency in love and emotional stability. Little Meg had been crying all through the night, her bed knocking against a wall as she rocked her small body back and forth with the torment of a child desperately in need of the love and the touch and warm cuddling of a mother.

Every day was a lonely world of sameness, of soul-destroying cream-coloured walls with their high windows that so cruelly restricted these small children to seeing only patches of sky or the chimney tops of adjoining buildings.

Only a few kindly faces ever came near her. Meg remembered how she longed to be chosen by one of the couples who would come to choose a child. She longed to be taken, taken to a loving home where she would have someone to call *Mum* and someone to call *Dad*. But she was always passed by, always left behind to face more lonely days in that loveless institution.

But Meg survived, becoming strong, strong enough to win through. The day came when she was old enough to leave the orphanage and fend for herself. Meg was eighteen and working in a hotel when she first met Harry Butler. Now, as she lay on her bed, she could still see his face as clearly as the day she first met him; tall, rugged with dark hair and a smile that made her weak inside. For Meg and Harry, it was indeed, love at first sight. They swore their love for each other within a week of meeting and they married as soon as they could.

Meg sat up on the edge of the bed, picked the letter from the floor and went over to the window which gave her a low-level view out over the meadow. The old farm building ruins at the edge of the meadow, stared biblical beneath the glaring Full Moon as it rose in the eastern sky, following the sun which had already vanished below the western horizon, like some giant celestial clock.

Meg's eyes were drawn, fixing on the old farm building. She had finished with tears long before. There was no point in crying any more. It was as if crying were a drug to which she had become immune. There had been a Full Moon, she recalled, a big bright moon on the night when Harry, her beloved Harry, was killed in a road accident.

They had been married for less than a year and the total time they had spent together amounted to just one year and a day. A period of three hundred and sixty-six days out of all the days of her life was all the happiness and love she had ever known. After Harry's death, she could never recover.

Now, life had kicked her once again. The letter in her hand was the last of a long correspondence, informing her that there was no possibility of ever tracing her mother, her father or any siblings or half siblings who might have existed. Meg stood at the window, her eyes glazed, fixed in a trance, blankly staring out across the moonlit meadow towards the old farm building which seemed to lurk in its own dark shadows.

She had been saving a half bottle of whiskey since Christmas, the only time she ever took a drink, when she needed it most. Christmas: a time when everyone else had family and friends and were not afraid of their memories or lonely dreams of what might have been. Christmas: a time when families were the central plank of Christian existence, and the lack of a family of her own, crushed Meg's fragile spirit.

Now, Meg was drawn to the bottle, even though she knew very well from past experiences that it would make her feel ten times worse, but at least she would fall asleep quickly and if she was lucky, she hoped, she might not wake up.

She took the bottle from behind a pile of neatly folded clothes on the top shelf of a cupboard. The cork slipped from her fingers and rolled under the bed as she put the bottle to her lips, tipped it back and gulped until every drop had been swallowed.

She looked at the Moon again. It was higher in the sky now, appearing smaller than it had earlier. She stooped beside her bed, pulling an old leather travelling case from beneath it. The dusty frayed straps were still fastened in their buckles, stiff after years of not being opened. The rollers on the buckles squeaked as Meg broke the old rusty seal. She pulled the straps free and opened the case.

She gazed at the contents which she hadn't looked at since the time of her Harry's death. She removed the top layers of newspaper which she had stuffed in as packing. Then she picked up the framed wedding photograph of her young self with her handsome husband. She studied it, timidly running her middle finger over the image of Harry's face. She closed her eyes, wishing, praying, hoping that by some freak of nature, he would appear before her and wrap his arms round her, putting an end to the awful, relentless misery inside her. A ribbon protruded from a wrapping of white tissue paper. Meg pulled it gently, unravelling the bow she had made all those years before. She pulled the tissue paper apart to reveal the wedding dress she had worn on her day of happiness. How deliriously happy she had been. How she dressed alone without a female friend to support her. But that didn't matter, didn't matter at all, because she was already the happiest woman alive and she and Harry were going to be together forever, a princess and her handsome prince.

Meg danced around the bedroom, holding her wedding picture close to her bosom. She undressed, letting her drab work clothes and underwear fall to the floor. She slipped into her wedding underwear and sat on the bed pulling her white stockings along her pale slender legs. She thought of the hotel room where Harry had undressed her for the first time, the first time she had ever been naked before a man.

The drink was taking effect and the room seemed to spin as she imagined Harry was there with her. He was standing there by the window, wanting her to look out across the meadow. The old farm building beckoned, its crumbling white walls outlined beneath the pale moonlight. Harry was with her. Then he was in the meadow calling her, wanting her to join him and he would be waiting for her in the old farm building where local children often played. She opened the bedroom door and walked along to another door that opened to a short path and to the meadow and away from Caqueux House.

A nebulous form hovered by the old farm building. Meg stopped for a moment in the meadow, oblivious to the damp grass beneath her feet. She cried out.

"Wait, wait. Harry! I'm coming. Oh, please wait!"

She plucked the skirt of her dress with both hands and ran as fast as her legs could run, run to her beloved Harry. Now she was among the old ruins where the boys played, her dress floating ghostlike in the moonlight. She called out again. "Harry, Harry." There was no answer only the old walls; silent and morbid around her. And then she saw it, a rope, which the boys had left, hanging over a door lintel above an arrangement of stones and bricks, one of their cowboy games.

It had been made into a hangman's noose, just like they had seen in the cowboy films.

Meg stood there, looking at the noose, her eyes fixed as it made a foreboding shadow against the pale moonlit wall. A voice kept telling her to go ahead and then all her pain would be over. Another voice was telling her to run, run away from this place and to keep on running and to make some kind of happiness for herself, somewhere else.

But Meg Butler was all out of run and all out of will-power. Her heart had been crushed, unable to even know any longer what hope or prayer was. Drowsy, she swayed, trying to keep her balance. She looked up at the Moon. It seemed sorrowful, melancholic, sadly suspended, trapped in its never-ending orbit around its parent, Earth.

"You're like me." She said, talking to the Moon. "You're just like me, a lonely pathetic existence with nothing to live for."

A voice whispered. "Come on, come over and join me. I have been waiting for you all these years. We will be together at last, together forever."

She looked at the rope with its gaping noose. It just hung there, motionless in the cool night air. It became Harry's face. He smiled, as he had so often smiled in her dreams. The vision began to fade and Meg in her madness moved forward to follow it. She swayed as she stepped onto the arrangement of stones and bricks. She reached for the rope and put the noose over her head.

The wailing noise screamed again over the meadow and the woods, disturbing animals and unsettling geese and ducks around the lake.

* * *

Josh Cogan rose with the sun. A cup of tea and he was, as usual, away across the meadow giving his dog, Jake, an early morning run. The air was fresh, and the new sun warmed his face. His eyes fixed for a moment on a piece of white cloth near to a clump of nettles. Josh picked it from the ground. It was a woman's handkerchief, still smelling of mothballs, still pristine, except for the dampness caused by the dewy night air. He wondered how it got there and who might have owned it.

Jake ran ahead, yapping and barking, towards the *Alamo* and Josh followed. Suddenly, he stopped dead in his tracks.

"Holy mother of god." He cried out as he saw the small body hanging lifeless above the earthy floor. He froze, before the bizarre, eerie sight of a bride in white, all ready for her wedding but on whom life and God, or perhaps the antilife and the Antichrist, had played a rotten cruel trick. He didn't recognise her at first. The face looked to be that of a youngish woman, made witchlike by the long grey hair which had become entangled in the rope. Her small white stockinged feet, dotted with flecks of dirt, pointed downwards and small dormant hands hung limp below straightened arms. Josh stood there, not really knowing what to do but he could see that it was all too late to do anything for this unfortunate woman.

He stepped forward for a closer look, gulping a dry swallow as he recognised the face. "Oh my God. Megs." He muttered. He hadn't realised until that moment that Meg wasn't a very old woman at all, middle-aged, not more than fifty, if that. She had a beauty that he had never seen before or never noticed. Somehow death, even such a sad and violent one, had rejuvenated her face, as if whatever had been ailing his servant woman all these long years had suddenly been allowed to drain away.

The rural peace was broken by the sirens of Garda cars as they sped along the country lanes towards Caqueux House. Meg's frail little body was cut down with little ceremony and laid on the ground. After a brief examination, two men lifted the body onto a stretcher, covered it with a blanket and slid it into the back of an ambulance.

* * *

A dribble of half-cooked egg-white oozed down the shell as Josh Cogan sliced the top from his boiled egg. The old kitchen was silent now, lifeless. Everything was just as he had left it earlier that morning. His knife and fork, his plate, his cup and saucer, a jar of strawberry jam, the sugar bowl, everything was still in the same place where he had left it …. mere lifeless objects with neither will nor personality, all adding to the monotony and the loneliness of his life.

Josh was missing Meg. There had never been anything between them, physically or emotionally. How could there have been. Both had been somewhat reclusive, existing on their own memories, living some other life. Neither had ever made any attempt to be attractive to the other. But he had developed a kind of fondness for her. He had become used to having her around, someone else in an otherwise lifeless house. He knew himself, that he was useless around the house and as they say, he couldn't even boil an egg.

It was tea-time. Josh's umpteenth slimy boiled egg, and he had not eaten a decent meal since Meg died. He looked around the old kitchen. The black range stood there in its dark recess, lifeless without a homely, warming fire. It used to be so welcoming, and Meg had so diligently kept it stoked-up, even in summer. Now, the house had become untidy, no one to clear-up after him, no one to wash and iron his clothes and no one to keep clean and tidy for. No one in the house except himself .... no one else at all.

Although Meg used to go about her chores with a saintly silence, Josh was always aware of her presence, someone picking up this and tidying that, opening and closing doors. Someone saying *good morning* and saying *good night*. He never knew much about Meg. She had come to work for his parents, just after the Second World War or the Emergency as it was known, with good references from the orphanage and from the hotel where she had worked. She was given employment, and no one ever questioned her after that. She never tried to get close to or interfere in Josh's life, took only a few days off each year and in all the time she had lived and worked at Caqueux House, she never had any visitors. Josh never knew about her inner torment, and she knew little about his private life and if they did get to know anything about each other, well, they just kept it to themselves.

Josh finished his miserable egg, drank two cups of tea and went off to O'Connor's for a few pints. Whenever he could, he would walk to the pub in Ballynamarbh, preferring to leave his car at home. It was always a pleasant walk, in fair weather, and it gave him an opportunity to chat with any of the neighbours he might meet on the road.

Josh always sat on the same bar stool at O'Connor's. He would talk to anyone who happened to be sitting near to him at the bar. It was a place where the locals could pass the evenings, sorting out the problems of the world and occasionally playing a game of darts. The dark brown timbers, the smoke-stained ceiling and the old stone floor all contributed to an atmosphere of old culture and old ways.

"They say there's an evil on your land." Said one old boy who was on a stool further along the bar from Josh.

"And what might that be?" Said Josh.

"Ah, ya know." The old boy shrugged. "They say animals won't go near the old place where Meg Butler died. They say the banshee can be heard there often."

"Well, the banshee hasn't wailed for me yet." Said Josh, pausing for a good moment as he held a flaming match to his pipe before drawing pensively on it, leaving the other drinkers waiting for a further utterance. Puffs of dense sweet-smelling tobacco smoke swirled in the air as he took the pipe from his mouth.

"Don't you be listening to all that aul talk now." Said Josh. "Can't ya leave the poor woman to rest in peace?"

A momentary silence followed as the drinkers digested what had been said.

"Still," said the old boy, "it wouldn't do ya any harm to have a word with Father Philpott."

"I'll not have any of that old hocus pocus on my land." Said Josh, annoyed at the interference.

It was after eleven when Josh left the pub. Garda Keane was on his beat, lingering here and there with his torch. Josh saluted him.

"Good night." He said.

Keane nodded appreciatively. "Good night to you, sir."

Quiet sort of fellow, Josh thought as he walked down towards the railway bridge. Ballynamarbh had that rural night stillness and peace about it. Most people were tucked up in their beds with only the occasional set of glaring headlights, rumbling along the main street. His footsteps echoed in the arched structure as he walked beneath the bridge. He had a feeling that he was being watched. He slowed his walk and half turning his head, he listened, his ears more alert than his eyes in the dark. Stupid, he thought, coughing to clear his throat, the sound of which echoed around him in the dark emptiness of the stone arch.

Half an hour or so later, Josh was walking along the gravelled driveway towards his front door. The tall trees stood silent, black and shadowy against the night sky. The feeling, that someone was watching him, came again. He looked around but he couldn't see anyone. Were the silhouetted tall trees and the hedgerows silently watching over him or were they conspiring to hide some evil monster that, at any moment, would spring out and grab him by the throat. *Must be the drink,* he told himself .... *the demon drink!*

Things were just as he had left them a few hours before. The lonely silence interrupted only by the monotonous tick-tock, tick-tock of the grandfather clock which stood, for as long as he could remember, in his entrance hall, beside the stairs. The stairs creaked in the same places as they did every night. He used the toilet, cleaned his teeth, undressed, switched out the light and climbed into bed. He lay there wide awake, looking at the clouds as they passed across the window-framed night sky. Josh was agitated, lonely, annoyed with himself. He wondered how, at the age of fifty, he had come to this state of affairs. He acknowledged his loneliness, telling himself that it was his own fault that he was still single and alone because that was always the way he had wanted things to be. He remembered the first time he made love with a woman. He had run off to London to find some excitement and to get away from his domineering parents who seemed to conspire with the overpowering religious society that seemed to want to control his very thoughts.

It was in a pub in Hammersmith where he met his first conquest. She was older than he was, with a playful twinkle in her eyes. Lilly, her name was. He was surprised at how much she liked his Irish accent, how it seemed to excite her and how it prompted him to exaggerate his Irishness, putting on a wildish *Paddy* act, to woo his English audience. He remembered his first words to her, joking that he was a poor Irish fella who'd never been with a woman and was desperately in need of the experience. He smiled as he remembered how she went along with his clowning and how, in front of his new English pals, she pulled him close to her and kissed him full on the lips. As a young man with a severe religious upbringing, he couldn't believe that life could have so much fun and happiness.

Lilly had a room not far from the pub. The clowning had deserted Josh as he stood in her doorway, looking shy and out of his depth. She took his hand and led him inside. He remembered the physical excitement of being alone with a woman who was quite obviously going to take him to bed. As they stood next to her bed, they gazed into each other's eyes. Now, they were gentle, silent, touching, looking, excited and not thinking about tomorrow.

Josh was asleep now, if you could call it sleep. His other torment had become a regular visitor of late, the torment that brought him back to the war, back to the last winter of the war. He could still feel the cold, an intense cold, as his unit battled for ground. The white blinding snow, four; five feet deep in places, covered the countryside. He had fired his rifle at the enemy before but had never seen them close-up. This was different. Now he came face to face with the enemy. The enemy! Who was the enemy? Some *foreign looking foreigner* who spoke only a word or two of English? Did the enemy laugh? Did they tell jokes? Did they listen to music? Did they love anyone? Did anyone love them? Josh soon found out about the enemy on the day he came face to face with a German soldier.

That face came once more into his dreams, into his head, into his mind, haunting him as it had done so often since the war. The pleading half-smile set beneath that distinctive Teutonic helmet. He remembered so clearly that brief few seconds. Two men who had never met before and in the blink of an eye, one would obliterate the other. Josh had often tried to rationalise it, telling himself that it was either his own life or the German's life. But that didn't help him forget the face that seemed to stare at him forever, the face at close range, the smiling face, the face that maybe, perhaps, might have been about to surrender. Suddenly it was all over. Josh pulled the trigger. He shot the German soldier, killed him or murdered him, ended his life. The picture was forever in his mind: the enemy soldier with a face, falling to the ground, a spurt of his bright red human blood spoiling the pure white snow.

He had to take cover beside the body of the man he had just killed. The body just lay there in the snow, the eyes still open and the blood trickling through his military greatcoat. Josh vomited. *How bloody final it all was!* .... He thought .... *so horribly, bloody final!*

His dream was vivid. He was praying, pleading .... *Jesus, help me* .... *Jesus, help me,* over and over again. *Jesus, help me* .... *Jesus, help me.* Josh was running, running away from the terrible carnage, through the snow at first, he was wading, panting gasping, trying to get away from that awful nightmare. The snowy landscape gave way to desert, hot shimmering air and sand. A man stood with his back to Josh, a man wearing a long white flowing robe. Josh called out .... *Jesus, dear Jesus.* The man turned to answer. Josh froze, petrified as the smiling face beneath a German war helmet fixed his terrifying gaze on Josh.

Josh sat bolt upright in the bed. His heart was pounding, the blankets and sheets, a twisted mess like his tormented mind. He buried his face in both hands, trying to clear his head.

Daylight came. Josh didn't want to leave his bed, but he didn't want to stay there either. Another day of working on the farm, well at least that was something to be grateful for, he supposed. He thought again about the state of his life with no offspring. No son for him to watch through childhood, through boyhood to manhood. He might have had grandchildren by now. Most men of his age were looking forward to ending their days playing with their children's children and taking things easy. But not for him, he thought. Now, he faced an endless round of sameness and no one with whom he could share his life.

Tea, bread and jam were all he could be bothered to do for breakfast. Old Jake didn't do much better, yesterday's cold tea poured over doorstep sized chunks of bread. The old dog lapped at his tray of food as if he never gave a thought for any other creature. When they had finished, they headed off to see that his cattle were all where they were supposed to be.

* * *

The morning mist was clearing, revealing the blue sky as Josh and his dog walked across the meadow towards the field where the cattle were grazing. A shimmering blob of bright colours grew clearer as he went close by the *Alamo*. A woman was seated on a folding stool, a brush poised at a canvas which sat on an easel. Her long dark hair was tied back with a red ribbon. It was such a delightful sight but a difficult one for Josh to comprehend as the sight of poor old Meg, hanging limp and dead, came into his mind.

Jake got there first, yapping and sniffing around the artist. Josh arrived a few steps behind. He stood there looking over her shoulder for a few moments while, seemingly unconcerned, she completed a few brush strokes. She stopped, laid down her brush and turned towards him.

"Oh, hello I hope you don't mind me being on your land?"

"Not at all. You are very welcome." Said Josh. "I never though anyone would be interested in this old place.

"Everything has its beauty." She said as she stood to face him.

Josh was stunned by her beauty, sort of Mediterranean, he thought, a bronze complexion with perfect features framed with shining dark hair and her dark alluring eyes intelligently analysing him. She was young, he reckoned, early twenties, and spoke with an educated English accent.

"Emma Cavendish." She said, offering her hand.

Josh wiped his hand down his jacket, suddenly feeling a little inferior.

"Pleased to meet you .... Josh Cogan .... Are you enjoying your visit to Ireland?"

"Very much." She smiled. "I'm just touring around .... me, my paints and the scenery, wonderful scenery." She paused for a moment. Josh was enthralled. "Do you know if I might get some casual work around here?" She said.

"Depends." He said. "What can you do besides painting nice pictures?"

"Anything." She shrugged. "Farmwork, housework. "Anything so long as I can do my art in between."

Josh looked at his watch. "Tell you what, why don't you come over to the house at about midday. I'll be in for a cup of tea about then. I might just be able to help you. See the house over there." He pointed.

There was a noticeable spring in his step as he headed off to the field where the cattle were grazing. Even old Jake seemed a bit livelier now.

The work seemed to go easier that morning. Josh brought feed out to the cattle on the tractor and made sure that the water troughs were full. Then he drove around the perimeter of the farm, checking that all was secure. His last job of the morning was to collect the eggs from the henhouse and then he hurried into the house for his cup of tea. He wasn't so much concerned with the state of the kitchen and the rest of the house as he was with himself. *Better clean up.* He told himself as he felt the stubble on his chin. *Don't want to look like some of those decrepit old egits in O'Connor's, now do I… wouldn't it be gas if I turned up one night with a fine young thing on my arm and a fine young English thing at that. Give 'em something to talk about, that would!*

His face was still beaming as he shaved, excited at the thought of having a beautiful young woman to tea and even more excited at the thought of her coming to work in the house. A woman around the house, he thought and maybe …. well, who knows! He grinned into the mirror. *You old dog …. you. Not too old though. Still passable.* He said aloud as he combed his hair. He grinned again, happy about life, happier than he had been for years. *Fifty-year-old man and a fine young thing. Well, Jaysus! Stranger things have happened.*

His smile was further enhanced when he went downstairs, along the hall by the grandfather clock, and opened the kitchen door. There she was, already set to work. He stood in the open doorway watching as the young English woman stood by the sink with steaming clean crockery stacked up on the draining board beside her.

"I thought I'd make myself useful." She said, smiling. "Hope you don't mind."

"I suppose you've made the tea as well." He grinned, feeling twenty years younger by just looking at her.

Their mutual confidence was interrupted by the sight of a black Ford Anglia rolling into the farmyard and stopping by the kitchen window.

"I wonder what he wants?" Said Josh, as he watched Father Philpott stepping out of the car.

Josh opened the back door to meet his uninvited guest.

"Ah Father Philpott." He said.

The priest stepped into the kitchen, making it obvious that he wanted to know who Josh's lady guest was. Josh introduced them, mentioning that Emma Cavendish would be coming to work at the house for a while. They shook hands while staring suspiciously at each other for a moment longer than was polite. When the uncomfortable pause was over, the priest turned to Josh.

"Ah .... I was hoping to have a quick word. In private if I may?"

Hesitantly, Josh agreed and so he went out to the yard with the man in black, leaving the English woman in the kitchen.

"So how can I help you, Father?"

Father Philpott hesitated for a moment. "Well, it's a little delicate."

"Well, spit it out then." Said Josh.

"The old ruin in your meadow."

"What about it?" Said Josh, feeling irritated.

"Well, I'd like to perform a small ceremony there, if you wouldn't mind, just a small ceremony, a few prayers." Said Father Philpott, aware that Josh didn't have much time for anything religious.

Josh forced a smile. "Oh, I don't really mind, I suppose. Anything for a quiet life. Go ahead if it'll keep everyone happy. Just yourself though, I don't want a load of holy-Joes trapesing all over the place on their knees."

Father Philpott couldn't help but smile. "Don't worry, it'll be just myself. I can go over their right now."

"Whatever you want." Said Josh.

"Well, I'll get to it then …. Oh! The English woman. Will she be staying in the house with you?"

"Hopefully." Josh shrugged with a cheeky grin and knowing that that would annoy the priest.

The priest said nothing for he had no reply to such an answer, but he was thinking that this was not really acceptable behaviour, going against rural religious ways but he had got what he had come for and Josh Cogan's morals would be another day's work.

"Right, I'll get to work then." Said Father Philpott, taking a small black case from his car.

"See you later, Father." Said Josh, reinforcing within his own mind that his private life was absolutely his own business and no one else's. He went back into the kitchen.

"You'll have to get used to that sort of carry-on around here." He said to the English woman who had been working away in the kitchen.

"Used to what?" She said.

"Priests." He said with a tone of exasperation. "Ah, he's not a bad aul skin, I suppose. He thinks there's a ghost or something over in the meadow."

"And is there?" Said Emma.

Josh laughed. "Don't tell me that you believe in all that rubbish too?"

"Perhaps." She smiled.

"Anyway, I suppose we'd better talk terms." He said.

Emma Cavendish poured freshly brewed tea into clean cups on clean saucers on a clean uncluttered kitchen table.

* * *

It was Saturday morning; children's confession time at St Vincent's church in Ballynamarbh. Father Philpott lifted the curtain that covered the fretwork on the door to the confessional. About nine or ten more children to hear, he thought. He left the curtain fall back into place and he opened the hatch to his right.

"Bless me father, for I have sinned …."

It was uncomfortably stuffy in there as he listened to the trivial sins of the local children. He hadn't lost any of his enthusiasm for the children's moral well-being but when he'd already listened to over twenty *Bless me Father's* in one morning, well, anyone's nerves would begin to fray. He gave the penance, administered the blessing, closed that hatch and opened the other hatch on his left.

It was a boy's voice that came through this time. Father Philpott listened patiently to the opening patter before the boy recited his sins. There was the usual catalogue, lying, using bad language and disobedience and then there was a pause.

"What is it, boy?" Said Father Philpott.

"Emm… nothing, Father." Said the boy.

"Are you sure, boy?"

"Yes, Father."

"Then you will say three Hail Marys and pray that the Lord, Jesus Christ will guide you."

Alfie Dawes left the confessional, looking towards his pals, Pete and George who were waiting for their turn to cleanse their souls. Alfie shook his head, and his pals knew that he hadn't confessed their mutual mortal sin. Pete had already made up his mind not to confess anyway. George wasn't so sure, but in the event, he chickened out too. Sins of children such as telling lies, stealing apples, swearing and jealously were quite acceptable but anything else was dubious, to say the least. Venial sins were all right, but confessing to a mortal sin, well that was a different thing altogether.

The pews that had been full of children, emptied as the confessions progressed and Father Philpott slid the confessional hatch back for the last time that morning. There was an odd silence and a coldness.

"Well, my child. How long is it since your last confession?"

A girlish voice whispered in a low unnatural tone, frightening him. He sensed an evil there, right next to him and he immediately made the sign of the cross in the darkened confessional. He gripped the crucifix that hung from his rosary. The voice whispered an incoherent mumble as if it had been scrambled into some confusing jargon.

Father Philpott rushed from the confession box to see who was there. But there was no one there, just an empty confessional with a broken rosary; the beads and the crucifix scattered on the floor. He picked the beads and the crucifix from the floor and in the palm of his hand, he looked at them, thinking, wondering and invoking Jesus Christ, knowing that he might just have had an encounter with the Antichrist. He looked around the church. It was empty now, the holy statues silently looking down on the rows of pews with the crucifix standing guard over everything.

A dagger-like pain shot through his chest. He stumbled forward, reaching out to grab the back of a pew. Then he was on the floor, feeling the blood rushing away from his face. He could see them all around him now, the faces, the ghoulish, smirking faces as they closed in on their victim, scowling, laughing as he took his last breaths, his last frightening breaths. He managed to call out the name of Jesus Christ and then he closed his eyes and was dead.

Part Two

"Lot twenty-five ladies and gentlemen. An oil painting titled 'Blue Moon'. Now I must stress that the artist is not known but professional opinion speculates that it could be the work of a well-known nineteenth century Irish artist, but the risk is, as always, with the buyer."

George Murray fiddled with the gavel as he described the painting with a mention of some of the previous owners. Lot twenty-five was paraded before the bidders who had gathered in the auction rooms of Murray and Power in Dublin. It depicted a Full Moon, rising in the night sky, shedding its pale light onto a meadow. George's eyes scanned the interested faces that crowded the auction room.

"So, what am I bid? Ladies and gentlemen. Will anyone start me off with five thousand punts?"

A little man wearing a tweed suit and waistcoat, standing at the back of the room, nodded discreetly.

"I have five thousand punts." Said George. "Do I hear six? Will anyone give me six thousand punts?"

George's keen eyes picked out an aging hippy with a goatee beard and grey-blond hair, tied back in a ponytail. The old hippy flicked his rolled-up catalogue.

"I have six. Do I hear seven? Seven thousand punts from anyone?"

Less than a minute later the little man at the back of the room and the aging hippy had bid each other up to eighteen thousand punts, much to the surprise of the other bidders. It was an even greater surprise to George for he had recommended a reserve of only eight thousand punts. The room went silent as the bidding stopped with the hippy.

"Any advance on eighteen thousand punts?"

The faces were silent, curious. George fixed on the competing bidder but the little man in the tweed suit had finished.

"Eighteen thousand punts .... once. Eighteen thousand punts .... twice." George raised the gavel and was about to call out the selling price for the third and final time when a clear determined female voice called out.

"Twenty thousand punts."

A communal gasp came from the crowd, their heads turning in the direction of the voice that called this bold knockout bid. George's eyes gleamed at the woman in a grey suit with long dark hair which she had tied back in a ponytail.

"I have twenty thousand punts. Whoever the artist was then he must be feeling smug in his grave today. Any more bids?" George's eyes settled briefly on the two previous bidders who shook their heads in surrender. "Twenty thousand punts once …. twenty thousand punts twice …. twenty thousand punts" …. he knocked the gavel on the podium. "Sold to the lady in grey." He smiled at her.

At that very moment, the sound of the gavel seemed to ring through George's ears as if a switch had been thrown in his head. He paused, feeling slightly stupefied. The crowd didn't notice the momentary interlude. George stepped down from the podium, passing the gavel to his partner, Larry Power. Larry stepped up to the podium.

"Lot twenty-six …...."

Suddenly, for some reason that George couldn't fathom, the auction didn't seem to matter to him anymore. He needed air, needed to get out of there for a while. He left the auction rooms and crossed the street, taking little notice of the passing cars. Looking for some tranquillity, George went into the railed, tree-line green of one Dublin's fine Georgian squares.

It was peaceful now, an oasis of quiet shrubberies and flower beds, isolated from the city hubbub. A slight breeze cut along a pathway whipping up a miniature whirlwind of dust and unruly fallen leaves. George found a corner bench which caught the sun but not the breeze. He felt odd, weird. What was it? He wondered. Did he just have some sort of palpitation or middle age turn? *No!* he told himself. *I'm only forty-three, for god's sake. I'm healthy.* He shrugged and he was indeed happy and had been until then but suddenly he felt, well, not exactly unhappy but out of sorts, melancholic or something. He couldn't quite put his finger on it. It was as if he had crossed some invisible barrier or threshold and now, he was on a different level, in unknown territory.

He stayed on the park bench for a long while without a thought for the auction or his colleague and staff. A little robin bobbed about in the bushes next to him. He watched it for a while, thinking that he hadn't observed such a creature for ages, probably not since he was a boy. He leaned back on the bench and closed his eyes, feeling the warm sun on his face.

His thoughts brought him back over his life, not in any detail, just some of the events that stood out or which were never too far below the surface of his mind anyway. He remembered the arguments he had with his father as to whether he should continue his education and go to college or go off and get a job somewhere. Those long shouting matches seemed to go on and on.

He remembered his first day at work. How green he was, a gangly youth who's only worth was to be a messenger boy, delivering letters and urgent paperwork to the front desk of other offices. But those days were good. No responsibilities and plenty of rugby. He loved rugby and smiled as he told himself that he could have made it to the top, playing for

Ireland, the Lions, the Baa Baas. If only he hadn't been better at drinking, not that he was an alcoholic but the allure of the pub and a wild social life, for a young man, were hard to escape.

The craziest thing that George had ever done was giving up his job when he was about twenty-three. He had been fed-up for a while and gave his notice. He packed his bag and went off to Paris where he stayed for a week before bumming around Europe for a few months. He ran out of money and returned to Dublin.

He remembered the women he had been with over the years. Some of them, he preferred to forget. Those days were all over now. Now he had Lisa, the girl of his dreams with her long blond hair and eyes that melted him. But, but, but ....
he wasn't quite sure what. There as something, not so much missing as .... well, he couldn't quite put his finger on it. Maybe, he was just chicken, he told himself, afraid of settling down .... maybe.

George felt cold. He strained to look at his watch without taking his hand from his trouser pocket. His body jerked, panicking, as he took his hand from his pocket so he could see his watch properly......"Jesus, ten to five."

The sun had moved behind a canopy of tree-tops, leaving the bench in a cool shade. He was even more confused now. Had he been there on the bench the entire afternoon? He could never have fallen asleep like that, especially in a public place, could he. He felt nauseous, groggy from the sun.

He made his way back to the auction rooms knowing that he had let his partner and staff down.

Crumpled, well-thumbed catalogues lay discarded here and there on the empty chairs of the auction room. The porters were already sweeping up after the day's business. Larry's voice echoed across the room. "George! Where the hell have you been?" He marched purposefully across the floor, fixing on George.

"Larry, I'm so sorry. I felt a bit dizzy, and I had to go out for air. I must have fallen asleep on the bench in the green."

"Jesus George. Have you looked in the mirror? You look like a tomato. Have you been in the sun all this time?"

"I know, I'm sorry. How did the rest of the day go?"

Larry smiled. "Very good. Don't worry, everything has been wrapped up just fine. Come on, you look as if you could do with a few jars."

They sat at a corner table in a pub near to the office.

"How are you feeling now?" Said Larry, thinking that this episode was so unlike George.

"Oh, I'm fine." Said George. "Must be something I ate." But he still had that sort of stunned feeling which he could not explain, not even to himself.

* * *

A clap of thunder followed by a sudden downpour marked a brief interlude in the warm sunny spell that had settled over

Dublin and the East coast. George had all but forgotten the bit of a turn or whatever it was that happened to him the previous week. It was late Monday afternoon as he paced the floor at his office. Sally, his secretary, typed her last letters on the day.

"Going abroad for your holidays, Sally?" He said as he stretched casually to peer over a display board so that he could see through the window to the street outside.

"Er … yes." Said Sally, without looking up from her desk.

George's attention was taken by an aging blue Land Rover which was being parked on the opposite side of the street. The brake lights glowed briefly.

"Will that be all?" Said Sally.

George was curious about the man who stepped out of the Land Rover. Sally raised her voice.

"Do you need anything before I go, George?"

"Oh, I'm sorry, Sally. No, let you go on then. Have a nice evening."

"See you tomorrow then." Said Sally, as she took her shoulder bag and made for the door while a man's outline hulked through the frosted glass as she did.

Sally pulled the door back, stepping aside to allow the man in. She looked to see that George had seen him, said goodbye again and left.

The man from the Land Rover stood there. A few raindrops had settled on the shoulders of his jacket. He removed his tweed cap to reveal a head of thick wavy hair.

"Are you Mr Murray?"

"I am indeed." Said George, smiling as he clicked the latch on the frosted door to close the office for the night. "What can I do for you?"

"Hello, I'm Arthur Thwaites." I have a property and I need a valuation on it." He spoke as if he was an officer out of Sandhurst, refined, commanding, slightly arrogant.

"Please come in and sit down." Said George as he moved towards the back of the office where there was a round interviewing table. He motioned Thwaites to a chair.

George, ready with a writing pad and pen, sat opposite and passed a business card to the client who looked at it as if inspecting a passport at a border crossing. He slipped the card into the breast pocket of his jacket.

"I am here on behalf of my employer, Emma Cavendish."

George nodded his head, waiting for Thwaites to volunteer more information.

"I'll be honest with you, Mr Murray, I did advise her to use a local agent, but she insisted that your company was one of the best in Ireland, and she would like you to personally do the valuation."

"I see." Said George, amused.

"Look, I'm in rather a hurry. I have squeezed this call in on my way to another meeting. I'll give you the details. It's a property called Caqueux House, near Polglas."

"You're kidding." Said George.

"I beg your pardon." Said Thwaites with a surprised look on his face.

"I know the place. I lived near there as a kid. I played in the fields around Caqueux House. Don't remember anyone by the name of Cavendish though." George tapped his pen against his note pad. "Ah, I remember. It belonged to an old boy by the name of Cogan. I suppose he's long dead?"

"Well Miss Cavendish has been there since before I came."

"I see." Said George.

"Anyway, as I say, I'm pressed for time so could we get on with it."

"Oh, forgive me. Now, how much land is there?"

"Three hundred acres in all, including woodland of about eighty acres which is part of a greater woodland area. There are several farm buildings and of course the house itself."

"And the purpose of the valuation?" Said George.

"Her accountants want to know. Tax purposes, I suppose."

"Right. When can I come to inspect it?"

"Thursday of next week. You can contact me the day before. "

Thwaites rose abruptly from his seat and went towards the door giving George no further chance to ask questions.

"I'll leave it with you then." Said Thwaites. I presume your report will follow fairly quickly."

"I'll do my best. We're quite busy with other valuations right now."

George extended his hand and Thwaites responded. "Next Thursday then."

George was deep in thought as he watched Thwaites cross the street and climb back into the blue Land Rover. He didn't quite know what to make of Thwaites. Odd fellow, he thought. He went to Sally's desk and signed the letters she had typed for him. Her perfume lingered in the air, reminding him of the time they spent a weekend together. They had thought, at one stage, that they wanted to be together but after a disastrous two days in Killarney, they knew that they were mistaken. There were never any hard feelings between them over it and the subject was never mentioned again. The evening had arrived. He gathered the envelopes for mailing, locked the office and left.

Wisps of steam rose from the pavements and the road surfaces as the sun reappeared after another shower. Grafton Street was thronging with people as they left their offices, shops and other places of work to go to their cars, busses and trains. George remembered a time when the flocks of nubile young women where his every thought. He remembered how great it was to go drinking and dancing in downtown Dublin during his twenties. He caught a glimpse of his own reflection as he passed a shop window on Grafton Street and the lingering glance of a passing blond woman elated him as their eyes met. But all that was over now. The days of late nights and womanising were all in the past now. He turned off Grafton Street and went along a side street, stepping off the pavement at one stage to let an old man pass. The security shutters on the windows of Hall's Jewellers, had already been secured. He was relieved to see that the shutters on the door had not yet been rolled down. He pressed on the bell.

The sun blind moved back a few inches and a man's face peered through the gap. The door opened and George stepped inside.

"I thought you weren't going to show." Said the shop owner. "Come on in. Better late than never."

"Sorry for being late." Said George as he stepped inside. "Had a last-minute caller at the office."

The shop keeper closed and locked the door.

"How are you, Bob." Said George.

Bob smiled. "I'm in good form, thanks. Come on into the back room."

George followed as Bob weaved, through the islands of glass showcases, to a small office at the back.

"Take a seat." Said bob as he sat at the desk and took five small jewellery boxes from a drawer. He opened each one with a professional flair. "Are these the type you had in mind?"

George smiled. He looked at the display of engagement rings and picked out three.

"Yep. I think she'll go for one of those."

"Any woman would be thrilled to bits to be offered the choice of one of these rings and if I may say so, the lady is being offered the finest of gentlemen too."

George grinned his appreciation for the compliment.

"Can I take the three on appro?"

"Of course. Will you be able to return the ones not chosen, say in two days' time?"

"Yes." Said George.

George took a taxi back to the office. A quick freshen-up, a comb through his hair and he was ready, winking at himself in the mirror…..

"Licenced to thrill women and one woman in particular." He smirked.

It was a fine sunny evening, freshened by the afternoon showers. The roads had dried out with only a few small puddles left in pavement depressions. George weaved through the traffic as he drove south towards Monkstown, a suburb overlooking Dublin Bay and the Irish Sea. He slotted his prized tape of James Bond music into the player; a dangerous thing to do as he always found it hard to resist driving faster to the beat of the theme music. George was happy, happier than he'd ever been in his adult life.

Lisa's house was in a cul-de-sac, off the main road. George rounded a series of corners leading to the small exclusive development of town houses. Her car was parked in the driveway.

Lisa was slow to answer as George pressed the doorbell for a second time. He pressed the bell again, somewhat impatiently this time. A long moment passed, and the door opened.

"Surprise! Surprise!" He said.

Lisa was indeed surprised, and she looked it too. She stood there awkwardly, her hand defensively holding the door.

"Oh, didn't expect you."

"Well, can I come in then?"

George stepped inside. He stood on the green carpet that covered the hall and the stairs, sensing that something was wrong.

"What's wrong?" He said. "You look a bit pale."

He touched one side of her face with the tips of his fingers, pecking a kiss on the other side. Lisa trembled nervously.

"No, nothing." She said. "I was just having a lie down, fell asleep in the sun."

"I've a surprise for you." He said, smiling with a kind of relief as he put his hand into his jacket pocket to retrieve the small jewellery boxes. At that moment, a creaking sound came from upstairs.

"What was that?" He said as he looked up through the stairwell. He turned to Lisa. Her face was like that of a little girl who'd been caught using her mother's best make-up. A shuddering fearful realisation shot through George.

"Tell me it isn't true."

In his anger, he took her by the shoulders but quickly released her, then he hurried up the stairs. Violently, he pushed Lisa's bedroom door open.

"What the hell's going on here?" He shouted at the man who was hurriedly pulling on a pair of jeans.

Raged, George punched the man in the stomach, making him collapse onto the bed. For good measure he pushed his forearm along Lisa's dressing table, clearing it of the jumble of scent bottles and jars of cream and lipsticks and all the other girly things which at that moment he just wanted to destroy. Lisa could only watch from the bedroom door, hoping that George had finished, which he had. He stormed past her on his way out, all but jumping down the stairs and slamming the front door behind him. Tyres screeched as he sped off in anger.

It was some time before his heartbeat slowed. He had never, in his whole life, felt so angry or been so destructive with it and he thanked his lucky stars that he hadn't hit Lisa in his rage. As he calmed down, so he slowed the car. He was close to his own home. He stopped outside, untidily abandoning the car but instead of going into his apartment, he went to his local pub.

A large television screen loomed in a corner of the bar. George ordered a pint with a chaser and stayed at the bar for the entire evening, drowning his sorrows and making it obvious that he wanted to be left alone.

The following day was a total loss to George. He phoned his business partner, giving an excuse that he was ill, the flu, migraine, he didn't really care what he said. Then he went back to bed. After a few hours, the bright, warm sun had come around to shine into his room and directly onto his face, making him feel sick.

It was late afternoon when he finally did leave his bed. He stood by a window which had a view out over the bay and the Irish Sea. The car-ferry from Holyhead was approaching Dun

Laoghaire harbour. It reminded him of the previous summer when he took Lisa on a motoring holiday to France. How happy he was then; how happy they both were, a fast car, the girl he loved beside him and the open roads of France. He thought about the little cafés and the romantic restaurants and hotels where they stopped along the way. He could still see Lisa, sitting by candlelight, her arms and legs bronzed, sipping her wine and then he could hear her giggle. Lisa had an infectious school-girl giggle, especially after a few glasses of wine.

He remembered the time they made love beneath the stars on a deserted beach. How very much in love they were, in tune with each other. He remembered how they laughed and how they would act out famous film scenes. Lisa would love it when he did his James Bond act. He would call her *Moneypenny* and she would respond with a sigh …. *Oh James*.

George leaned his forehead against the window. He hadn't been physically injured, but his entire body felt racked by pain, as if his insides had been ripped out. Some relief came with the inevitable tears. They flowed warm, salty and childlike and were cold and irritating by the time they reached his chin.

Wallowing in self-pity, George blew his nose and took a bottle of whiskey back to bed. The evening was one of tears and drink, his emotions a mixture of anger, hurt, hatred and jealousy, love, forgiving, unforgiving and more hatred. How could he have been so stupid, so very stupid? How could she have done this? …. *little bitch*. Screwing with some dopy bastard who looked more like an arsehole .... *biggest arsehole ever! Well, he's welcome to her......*

The next day and night were more of the same. He didn't want to leave the apartment. He didn't want to face the world. He just wanted to bury his head under the pillow with the duvet wrapped tightly around him. The drawn curtains kept the light away, the light that said that the rest of the world was awake and alive. Everyone else was living and getting on with their lives. George felt safe in the warm darkness of his bed, cut off from the world which could disappear into some cosmic black hole for all he cared.

Whenever the phone rang, he just left it ring. If it was Lisa, then he just didn't want to know. Well, he did but he didn't. *Let her stew. Let her go to hell.*

By evening he had had enough. Enough drink, enough crying but most of all he had had enough self-pity. He stood in front of the full-length mirror. His dishevelled shorts, tossed hair, unshaven face with reddened eyes, made a pathetic sight.

"Ok, George Murray! You've been down this bloody awful road before. Where did it get you? You've already lost two years of your life grieving over women. Women you would have given your life for at the time. But you let them know it and they took full advantage of your love. Your own stupid fault. You handed yourself to them on a plate. It got you only heartache and more heartache. So, no more of this. Do you hear me, you stupid bastard!" He pointed to himself in the mirror as if scolding a wayward child. *"Now come on. No more Mr Nice Guy..... That's*

it, George Murray….. No more shit. Got that, ya stupid idiot."
He shouted at his own reflection, daring himself to be strong.
He managed a smile with his new-found determination,
knowing in his heart that it was easier said than done but it
made him feel better, for the moment at least.

The soothing hot water beat off his shoulders as he stood
under the shower. He stayed there for several minutes,
allowing the jets of water to blast the pain away. He
remembered a time when he was only about seven or eight
and had been sent to stay with his grandparents who lived
about thirty miles from Ballynamarbh. How he had looked
forward to the trip for weeks with the promise of exploring
their farm and with a pony too. He remembered that pony
so well.

His father drove him to his grandparents' farm, one Sunday
afternoon and he remembered that sudden awful lump in his
throat, reality dawning, as he watched his father drive away.
He had never felt home-sickness before. He didn't know what
it was at the time except that it hurt something awful. It was
a wrenching pain from deep down in his stomach. When his
grandfather found him crying in the barn. He remembered
how the gentle old man put his huge arm around him, giving
him a cuddle with words of wisdom that had stayed in his
mind ever since.

*"This won't be the last time that life will seem hard to you but
whenever it does then what you have to think of is that it will
pass, and in the meantime, have a good wash, put on some clean*

clothes and polish your shoes. Always makes you feel better after a wash and clean up …. always."

Now, after all those years, George could still hear his grandfather's voice, gently but firmly giving life-saving words of wisdom. He dressed; clean, fresh clothes of course and polished shoes and the thought struck him that most children now wore trainers and runners and had probably never worn a pair of leather shoes, never mind being able to polish them

Hot sweet tea with toast and a couple of headache pills made George feel a little better. After a walk by the seafront that evening, he was a new man …. well …. almost.

It was twilight when George returned home. An envelope had been dropped through his letter box. A dull hangover pain shot through his head as he bent down to pick it from the floor. He recognised Lisa's handwriting along with the faint whiff of her trademark perfume. Determined not to give in, he crossed out his name and readdressed the envelope without opening it and threw it on the hall table, intending to post it on his way to work the next morning.

Bob was his usual discreet self when George returned the rings. He was being careful not to hurt George's feelings. George did feel obliged to offer an explanation of some sort but didn't really want to go into the whole debacle, merely saying that he couldn't win them all and left it at that.

"Maybe it just wasn't meant to be." Said Bob.

George smiled. "Thanks anyway, Bob."

He bade Bob goodbye, triggering the shop doorbell as he left.

George was relieved to find the staff busy when he went back to the office. He couldn't help wondering if any of them knew about what had been happening in his private life. They moved within the same social circles and if one of them knew about Lisa's affair then surely, they would all know. He made straight for Larry's office.

Larry and George were not only business partners but had become good friends too and they both knew that they could confide in each other on such occasions. George paced back and forth as he told Larry about Lisa. Larry just listened. That was all he thought he could do. This was also the day that George was to go to Ballyamarbh.

"Anything I can do?" Said Larry.

George shook his head. "Thanks, but I'll be fine …. It will do me good to get away for a while. I will let you know."

"Well, do let us know where you are. You might let Sally know where you are staying. Yes, it will be no harm for you to get away." Said Larry.

Sally was stretching into the top drawer of a filing cabinet when George came out of Larry's office. He stepped close to her. Startled, she turned abruptly.

"Oh, I'm sorry." She said as they almost bumped into each other, momentarily exchanging an awkward glance. Efficient as ever, Sally noted George's destination in her desk diary, and he was to let her know the hotel where he would be staying when he found one in or near Ballynamarbh.

* * *

It was cloudy as George drove southwest away from Dublin that morning. He fiddled with the radio buttons, but he couldn't find a programme he liked. If it was not some heavy metal or punk rock, then the choice was discussions on mundane topics like social security or some other voice droning on about God knows what. Annoyed, he shoved an Elvis tape into the slot. His mind, however, was still thinking about Lisa. He wasn't going to be able to forget about her that easily.

He focussed his thoughts on Caqueux House and inevitably his mind wandered back to his childhood friends, Alfie and Pete. He had not laid eyes on them since that last summer when they played together in the *Alamo*. He remembered or thought he remembered how they seemed to have spent nearly all their free time at the *Alamo*. Then George's family moved to Dublin when his father took a job there. George never kept in touch with his old pals. They just split up and that was that.

Lisa was on his mind again, making him aware that he still wasn't married but he told himself that there was no harm in that. He had often thought about getting married, but he didn't want to do it just for the sake of social conformity.

Somehow, settling down had eluded him and now it seemed that he never would.

He remembered his first love at seventeen. It lasted a mere three months and he was crazy about her; a girl called Yvonne. She was petite and very feminine. That was what appealed to him most. He could still see her face. They say you never forget your first love. She had soft yellowy hair which rested on her shoulders and her fringe gave her eyes a certain allure which made him want her even more. It was the first time he'd ever undone a bra and he remembered being chuffed of the fact that he didn't fumble, knowing instinctively how it was done and then after that he was able to do it with one hand.

Since then, he'd felt quite a few women's breasts. He tried to count the number of women he had bedded over the years. He lost count after about fourteen or fifteen. The first half dozen or so, were easy to remember, as were his most recent conquests. But it was those women in-between who were the most difficult to remember. He smiled to himself, reckoning that the number could be as high as two hundred. *Naw, more like three hundred,* he joked with himself. But there were some awful bitches there too, women he never wanted to see or hear from again.

The worst kind of women were those who were sad in themselves, women who had drink taken ..... the worst, definitely the worst, the most dangerous, he thought. One minute they would be all over you, all amorous the next they would be in floods of tears and blaming men, all men for all their troubles. If you happen to be the only unfortunate man around then they would let you have it, with hysterical accusations of using them and all sorts of trickery. Ah! Women, George said to himself, some of them could be bad bitches when they wanted to.

His journey to Ballynamarbh took him across the Curragh in County Kildare. He caught a glimpse of a lone racehorse being schooled between the grassy undulations. The Elvis tape had finished and again, he pressed the buttons to find something he liked on the radio. At last, he found a station that was playing his kind of music. Something he could relate to, something that would suit his melancholic mood. George wasn't in a hurry. He stopped at a pub for a plate of sandwiches and stayed for a while, lingering over a pot of coffee as he watched people coming and going.

Later in the afternoon, he reached the country town of Polglas, deciding to drive through it rather than taking the bypass. It seemed not to have changed much since he was a boy but then he had to admit that he couldn't have known Polglas as well as he knew Ballynamarbh. A sprawl of new houses had spread out to the north of the town which before had been open countryside. The traffic, of course, had increased and the nearer he went towards the town centre, the heavier the traffic became. Like many other towns, Polglas hadn't escaped this late twentieth century scourge; with trucks, vans, cars, all choking the old town to a state which previous generations could never have imagined.

With frayed patience, George passed through Polglas. Ballynamarbh was just a few miles down the road now. Signposts informed him that it had also been bypassed with a new dual carriageway. The old road had been left to serve the old village, as it had done through the centuries of cattle droving and horses pulling carts and the days when most people only ever ventured as far as the next village or to a nearby town. Dangerous curves and long sweeping bends remained, challenging his male psyche to an exhibition of driving skills. The thought struck George that he was only a boy when he had last been along this road and he certainly wasn't able to drive then.

Almost there, just a few more bends, he reckoned. Fresh cow dung on the road was a sign that he should slow down and just in time too. Had he been doing the James Bond, then he surely would have mown down at least five of the beasts from the heard that suddenly appeared as he rounded a bend. Still, George burned an uncivilized amount of rubber as he screeched to a stop. He switched off his engine, deciding that he was better off enjoying the wait, as the herd of cattle passed by; some brushing their wide bellies against his car. The dense bovine faces moved slowly past. The cows' faces were level with his own face. He was thinking that they were lucky that they didn't think, didn't worry about anything and didn't even know that they had miserable lives. Now that's happiness, he thought.

The rural procession passed by. A thickset, ruddy-faced farmer and a teenage girl nodded appreciatively to George as they urged their dumb but contented charges forwards with their big knotty sticks. The road ahead was clear but now with a covering of fresh cow pats. George drove on, trying to dodge the cow dung. Another few bends and he saw the speed limit signs marking the beginning of Ballynamarbh.

The road brought him along the top of the village where he stopped on the wide sweep of hard shoulder at the Catholic church. His memories of St Vincent's were very vivid now. This was the church where he used to go to Mass and confession, the place where his identity was formed. He looked down the incline of the main street towards the railway bridge at the very bottom of the village. Nostalgia tingled inside him as he thought about those boyhood days.

George stepped out of the car and onto the gritty roadside by the church. The warming sun was still high. No need for a jacket, he thought as he locked the car and walked. He looked at the church which dominated the village. Beneath the spire, the hands on the weather-worn clock with its weather-worn Roman numerals, had given up, settling for eternity at half past six. The walls had been rendered with a drab grey pebbledash which was crumbling in places. Veiny ivy vines were taking hold wherever they could. The lych-gate which he had remembered was not there, the quaint piece of bygone craftsmanship had been replaced by an ugly opening with a levelling of grit and tar. George pondered this piece of official vandalism.

The gritty forecourt led to a path which took him through the old churchyard. Time and neglect had taken its toll. The old headstones stood wearily among the depressions and the weeds. Many were tilting at uncomfortable angles as if they knew that just like their bony charges beneath them, they too would soon succumb to time and simply topple over. A scattering of old crows squawked mournfully as if it was their job to make death and even life, miserable.

The open church porch invited George to go inside. It was more for old time's sake or maybe because of some religiously induced lifelong habit that he dipped the tip of his right, middle finger into the holy water font and blessed himself. He hadn't done that for ages and felt a little fraudulent. As a child, he would bless himself with all the saintly reverence that the nuns had drummed into him. The awkward, heavy inner door creaked as he pushed against it and stepped inside.

Shafts of bright sunlight lit-up the rows of empty pews, all solemnly awaiting their congregation. The altar dominated, but it too looked somewhat lonely as if waiting for the faithful or a priest or someone to turn up and make its existence worthwhile. It all seemed smaller than he remembered or thought he remembered. A tray of burning candles flickered bright before a statue of the Virgin Mary, each flame a request .... *to cure an illness* .... *for a good harvest* .... *to help someone pass their exams* .... *to stop the suffering in the world* .... *for the poor souls in Purgatory* .... *a thank you for helping me* .... *a thank you for my health and strength* ....

George sat into a pew by the aisle thinking about his first confession. The nuns had been preparing his class for months. He could see himself as a child sitting there, waiting for his turn to go into that dark, secretive place. He had been instructed that he should kneel and with joined hands, confess his sins to the priest and to God. He had rehearsed his sins in his mind, telling lies; three times, disobedience; twice, using bad language; once. For all that, his first penance was only one Hail Mary. He remembered thinking that penance was easy. He had been let off lightly and he had a good feeling of being cleansed or released from some burden or something. He remembered feeling lighter on his feet as he left the confessional.

George hadn't been to confession since he was a teenager, but he had to admit that it could be a useful catharsis, a therapy of some sort. Life was simple in those days, he thought. People still had respect for each other and for their little part of the world. Now the mood was to throw away thousands of years of accumulated wisdom within a generation or so, the clowns were taking over the circus or was it that the sinners were taking over the church.

He looked at the statue of the Virgin Mary, wondering if there really was an after-life with a heaven and a hell? Was there a God? He could never really decide if he believed or not, but he did not want to believe that creation was just a random happening. He wanted to believe in a God and the Christian God was the one he was reared with but then again, he was never fully convinced.

A door slammed, sending an echo through the church, disturbing George's thoughts. A much overweight, woman wheezed unhealthily with the exertion of walking as she waddled along the aisle, her legs swollen with Elephantiasis. She made an even bigger commotion as she eased herself into a pew by the statue of the Virgin Mary. Poor woman, George thought, probably prayed all her life and all she gets is bad health. He looked at the tabernacle on the altar.... *Go on God, give her whatever she prays for.*

He remembered when as a small boy at mass he would watch as the priest opened the tabernacle. He used to think that it was the Holy of Holies, the very place where Christ himself lived. He would watch as the priest opened the miniature doors to reveal a shining golden chamber where no evil could ever exist. He smiled at his childhood memories, definite rights and wrongs. Good and bad were clearly defined, marked out. Now? Well, life was just one big free for all and you must fight your corner to make it and you have to fight even harder if you want more than mere existence.

The overweight lady struggled to her feet, dipped her fingers into her purse to find a coin which she dropped in the box and lit a candle. She blessed herself, turned and waddled back along the aisle. She smiled at George, a warm, homely smile which warranted only one response .... He smiled back.

He blessed himself again at the holy water font as he left the church. It was a little cooler outside now, so he took his jacket from the car and headed down into the village.

The school was still there and much as he remembered it with its low surrounding walls and railings. The windows had all been replaced and the playground seemed a brighter place with more colours and hanging baskets and shrubs and even some benches. Two bright blue portacabins, recent additions, looked out of place next to the old brick schoolhouse. George thought of his first day at school. He had been looking forward to it so much but how frightened he became when he discovered that his mother had left him there and how it seemed that he had been deserted and cheated. Whatever it was, it hurt. He cried for most of the morning.

When he was over all that, there was Peter Murphy. Peter Murphy, the Junior Infants' bully. George smiled at the thought of his first run-in with Peter. It was over an apple. George was happily munching on an apple in the school yard when Peter came along and just took it from him. George just stood there, looking at him without making any sort of protest. He watched, afraid as the bigger boy laughed, munching juicy mouthfuls of his apple.... His apple! George's parents had a conference about the bullying and his father took him into the garden that evening and taught him how to defend himself and to how to be devious about it. The next day George took his lunch box and went behind a tree. Sure enough, the bold Peter Murphy followed. George was still afraid but thought of what his father had told him. As the boy Murphy came in for the spoils, George grabbed him by the tie, pulling him forward, smashing an apple against the bully's mouth. George took the advantage and pushed him to the ground. Peter Murphy didn't bully George again but soon they were to become the best of friends. Funny old world! What had become of old Pete? Where was he now? George wondered.

He moved on from the school, walking further down into the village. Parked cars lined the street. When George was a kid only a handful of cars would be parked on the main street, old Austins, Hillmans, the big American-like Ford Zodiacs and Zephyrs. Nearly all of them, George seemed to remember, were either black or grey or some off-white colour. The old green post box was still there outside the Post Office, still at the same place where it had been for decades like some Toy Town character, eager to serve the people. The time will come when nobody knows what a post box or even what a letter is or was, he thought. George remembered the time when he went into the post office to cash a postal order for ten shillings, which his grandfather had sent as a birthday present. He could still feel the thrill of coming out of the post office with a nice, new, crispy, pink ten bob note.

A member of the Garda passed by as George looked around the street. He was a youngish policeman who nodded approvingly, and George nodded back. "Hello." George said. George walked on, seeing the grocery shop, still there, across the street. It used to be owned by the O'Neill's. It had been a real old country grocery shop where you could leave your list in the morning and your order would be ready that afternoon, all packed-up carefully in a cardboard box. He thought of the dark chocolate biscuits which were weighed out loose and put into a brown paper bag. Tea came in packets. No one had even heard of tea bags then. Oranges came wrapped individually in tissue paper and all together in a paper bag. Bread came from the baker, in a van, milk came in glass bottles with silver foil tops and cream was sold from the milkman's cool, dripping ladle. What had been O'Neill's, was now a small supermarket which had been extended into the adjacent buildings, to the left and to the right. The name *Fitzpatrick* blazoned in large red letters over the entrance. There was no sign of the hardware shop.

The Garda station was still there. A patrol car with mud flecks around the wheel arches was parked outside. George remembered Guard Keane and the other guards who were there when he was a boy. He could still see them as they went about on their bicycles, in their uncomfortable looking uniforms with the ends of their trouser legs held taught with bicycle clips. Everyone respected the police then and children even feared them, having had it instilled in them that respect for the law and the forces of the law were the same thing.

George was about eight, he reckoned when he was caught stealing apples from an orchard. He thought he had got away with it but just as he was climbing over the orchard wall, he felt a tugging at his collar. He froze, sick with fright at the sight of the man in blue demanding an explanation. Guard Keane seemed to play for a while, toying with George's fear and asking questions. George has visions of being thrown into gaol along with the awful shame and the rage of his father. But the village cop was a fair man. He let the kid off with a warning.

The pub, on the same side of the street as the post office, was now also a hotel. In the old days it was just a little village pub. It had been owned and run by the same family for decades and consisted only of a front bar and a small snug. It was an old man's pub where some of the clientele would spit on the floor, where the smoke from tobacco reeked in the air, where they swopped exaggerated stories about the war of independence and the ensuing civil war.

A couple of old warriors of the civil war used to frequent the pub on Friday and Saturday evenings. But one was a De Valera Man and the other was a Collins man. They would take their stools, one at one end of the bar and the other at the opposite end. They never actually spoke to one another but would occasionally hurl insults at each other by referring to each other as *that feckin Treaty fella* or *that bloody De Valera bastard*. It wasn't until they died that it became know that they were brothers, who were born and reared away out in West Kerry. Both men had been in love with the same woman, but she left Kerry, without any trace as to where she might have gone. The old soldiers heard that she was living near Ballynamarbh and so they followed her there and they never left. It seems that they took opposite sides in the civil war just to spite each other. They had, become trapped in their own tribal time warp, wallowing in old, exaggerated and imagined injustices and convinced by their own rhetoric.

George paused outside the hotel. The street curved slightly at the bottom before disappearing beneath the arched railway bridge. The railway line had been closed for years and the old track was now a country dirt-path.

George pushed at the glass door of the hotel and stepped into the foyer; a square area with rustic beams, cream-coloured walls and a red carpet. The fresh smell of polish gave him confidence that it might be ok to take a room there. A good sign, he thought. There was no one at the reception desk but he could hear voices coming from where he presumed to be the kitchen. He reached out, slapping the buzz-bell with the flat of his hand. Always wanted to do that, he thought with a smile. A few seconds passed before someone came along.

"Hello, can I help you?" Said the young woman.

George was guessing that she would be about twenty or twenty-one. He also noticed that she was very attractive with shoulder length red hair and a great figure.

"I'd like a room please. Anything available for tonight?"

"Just the one night?" She said, her distinct country accent reminding George of his mother's voice.

"Well, it might be a couple of nights, I don't know yet."

The receptionist consulted the diary.

"Yes, we have a single. Will that be ok?"

"Fine." Said George.

As she handed the key to him, George noticed her slender manicured fingers.

"Number twelve, up the stairs and along the corridor towards the end." She said, smiling.

George rested on the bed for about half an hour. Lisa was constantly on his mind. He didn't really want to think about her, but he couldn't help himself. He kept seeing that other man in her bedroom. It was playing over and over in his head. One minute he wanted to kill her and the next he just wanted her to appear there on the bed beside him and they would make love and fall asleep, content in each other's arms.

A refreshing shower made him ready for the evening. He was about to go into the bar for a drink when he remembered that he had left the car away up at the top of the street by the church. It was cool on the shaded side of the street, so he crossed over to the sunny side. The country village street was quiet with just one car passing during the time it took him to walk as far as the church.

The evening sun highlighted one side of the church. He hadn't, until now, noticed the field at the rear which had been annexed by the church for use as a graveyard. Modern white headstones glinted in the sun as it sank down towards the western horizon. His car sat alone where he had left it, beneath the trees. He could see a priest who was strolling near the old churchyard. George nodded acknowledgement to the priest who didn't respond and looked as if he was concentrating deeply on something or maybe he was saying his office. George sat into the car and drove down along the street to the hotel.

There were only three other people in the bar at the Shamrock Hotel. An elderly couple sat at a table in a corner, looking as if they had run out of conversation years before. An old codger sat comfortably at one end of the bar. Part of the furniture, George thought. A youthful looking barman who was cleaning glasses, looked up as George climbed onto a stool.

"Pint of Guinness, please." George said, conscious of raising his voice. The barman nodded, dropping the tea-towel onto a tray of upturned glasses. It took some time for the barman to fill the glass, letting the black liquid settle, topping it up again and letting that settle before topping it up once more. George took the opportunity to empty his pocket of loose change. The fistful of coins clanked noisily onto the counter. The noise gave the old codger an excuse to look at George as he separated the pennies from the silver, arranging them into neat stacks. The barman sat the pristine pint glass, of the precious chilled black stuff with its creamy head, onto a bar mat in front of George. The barman looked older close-up, about fortyish, George thought. He was smart and tidy with a professional air about him, a man proud of giving a good service.

"Thanks. What's the damage?" Said George, pointing to the change on the bar.

The barman selected and slid the coins across the bar with his fingertips until he had the correct amount.

"This old place has changed a bit since I was here last." Said George.

"And how long is that sir?"

"Oh, too long, makes me feel old. I lived here when I was a kid …. went to school up the road." He said, noticing the barman's name tag on his shirt pocket. "Liam, can I call you Liam?"

"Sure."

"I'm George. I'm staying here. Tell me, Liam, do the O'Connor family still own this place?"

Liam shook his head. "No. I'm here about five years now and the O'Driscolls bought the place about ten years ago."

The old codger at the other end of the bar was itching to get into the conversation so he made a fuss of carrying his empty glass the length of the bar to plonk it down before the barman for another pint.

"Same again?" Said Liam, knowing what the old codger wanted as he put a sparklingly clean pint glass to the dispenser.

"Business or pleasure?" Said the old codger, looking at George.

"Bit of both." George shrugged.

Neither said anything more for a few moments as if both were thinking of something intelligent to say or were trying to gauge the other's mentality. George broke the awkwardness.

"You're a local man." He said

"Yeh, you could say that." The old codger nodded as if acting out a lifetime of evasiveness.

"You know Miss Cavendish over in Caqueux House?" Said George.

The barman returned, placing a fresh pint on the bar in front of the old codger who hesitated expertly in attempting to pay. It worked.

"I'll get that." Said George, placing a crispy five punt note on the bar.

The old codger didn't argue as he lifted the pint to his lips, gulping as if a free drink was the Holy Grail of all boozers. The ceremonial gulping was followed by a contented sigh of satisfaction. He put the half full glass back onto the beer mat then wiped the froth from his lips with the back of his hand.

"Miss Cavendish? You mean the Contessa? He said with a wry smile.

George's eyes widened quizzically.

"Ah, she's not a real countess. We only call her that." Said the old codger.

"Why's that?" Said George.

"Ah, she's just a stuck up aul cow."

"She has a reputation then?"

"Yeh, you could say that. Good at sending husbands to the graveyard."

"Is she wealthy?" George asked.

The old codger took his time, taking another gulp of his pint and relishing the attention of his audience. Eventually he answered.

"Well, no one really knows the answer to that. She never gives a bob to any of the local charities. Seems to employ foreigners and not many of them at that. Mean aul cow and as for that Thwaites fella, her so called manager, the fecker's as bent as a Connemara road. Huh, him with his bloody upper-class accent. Major Arthur bloody Thwaites indeed. Bollocks!"

Another silence followed as they drank from their pint glasses.

"Dublin?" The old codger said, enquiring.

"I am that." Said George.

Sensing that there was no more free drink to be had from this session, the old codger slapped his empty glass on the bar and pushed his old bones off the stool, emphasising a painful effort.

"Well, I'll be off boy. Have a few jobs to do first thing."

The barman gave a knowing smile as they watched the old codger move cunningly towards the door.

George ate a fillet steak with a glass of red wine for his evening meal, but he found eating alone in a restaurant was more functional than enjoyable. He skipped desert and coffee.

There was still some daylight, so George went for a stroll. The village street was almost deserted with only a couple of women having what looked like a good old gossip on the pavement. He wondered why it was so quiet and why there were no children playing anywhere. Usually on these fine summer evenings there would always be a few kids here and there, playing or making mischief or just being noisy. Television, he thought .... Everyone just watches television nowadays.

George walked down the street towards the old railway bridge. The darkened stone arch with stalactite daggers poised above, seemed to mutter back to him in echoes as he cleared his throat. The sound of an approaching car disturbed his thoughts and he quickly moved aside as the horn hooted and the car sped through beneath the bridge.

Ballynamarbh ended at the bridge. The road swept in a large curve, parallel to the railway line for a while, through lush fields. A magnificent setting sun sprayed its orange light over the countryside. George climbed the railway embankment. It was steeper than he had remembered or maybe it was because he was no longer a boy when a climb such as this would be no problem at all. There was a time when he could run up the embankment and along the railway line without stopping. Now when he reached the old line, he had to pause for a moment to catch his breath. The track itself had been torn up leaving an elevated, dirt path receding into the distance.

He stood on the bridge where he could see the village and the church spire in amongst the trees. He remembered going into Polglas one Saturday afternoon with his boyhood pals, Alfie and Pete, to see the film, The Bridge on the River Kwai. He smiled as he remembered sneaking into the cinema without paying and how the three boys sat enthralled throughout the film. He hummed the tune of Colonel Bogey. Da da …da da da dum dum dum …. da da …. da da da dum dum …. imagining himself to be Alec Guinness marching along the bridge with his swagger stick, inspecting the work of his fellow prisoners of war.

George gazed along the disused railway line. He could see a grey rooftop with a chimney stack in the distance and reckoned that it must be Caqueux House. Lisa came to his mind again, not that she was ever very far from his thoughts. He wondered what she was doing at that moment. Then he thought about her new friend. He shuddered, mentally killing the subject.

He kept on walking away from Ballynamarbh, out into the countryside, just as he had done so often when he was a kid in short pants and sandals, skipping along over the splintery sleepers. He wondered about time and about how unforgiving and unrelenting its passing is. He remembered the lines of Kipling …. *the unforgiving minute* …. What became to his boyhood pals, Alfie and Pete? He was trying to pitch himself back into his boyhood, back into the past.

In the fading light, small shadowy figures danced on the weedy path before him. Rabbits, he reckoned. The sun had not fully gone away yet. The countryside was tranquil in its wake. The lake came into view, the lake where they used to fish, now shimmering and silvery in the twilight. Wearing his slight city shoes, he was trying to avoid stepping on any sharp stones, once the bedding for the mighty railway sleepers.

The woods came into view, and he thought of *The Alamo*. *Golden days* ...... he said to himself ...... *golden days*.

As if on a pilgrimage, he branched off, leaving the railway path and then he walked by the edge of the woods. There was no path or dirt track here now. Kids of today, he thought, no sense of adventure. Television, that's all they know now. He remonstrated with himself for thinking that way as if he and his generation where the font of all wisdom.

It was turning darker now, twilight, as he cut through the woods, quiet, still, eerie. Twigs and bits of scrub creaked beneath his shoes. He felt as if he was trespassing on sacred ground or was it that he was trespassing on sacred memories, as if his past belonged a very different person, someone else! Must stop these crazy thoughts, he said to himself, too much living in the city. Must get back to nature. He stopped for a moment to pee.

The dark shadowy silence was making him feel vulnerable .... *Could drop down dead here and nobody would find me for weeks. That's if there would be anything left of me ....* George shuddered at the thought. He looked about, thinking that he heard a noise. Was there someone there? Don't be stupid, he thought. Then he heard it again. It was as if the air had spoken. A voice whispered. He stopped dead as if a hand had touched his right shoulder. *No,* he thought, taking the precaution of crossing himself. The whisper came again but stopped as he stopped walking. The drink, he thought, the demon drink, should have listened to my mother. He wondered why he invoked his mother just then. *The mind, always playing its tricks. Yeh, but your mind, George Murray, plays more tricks on you than anyone else's mind plays on themselves.* He told himself. And what the hell was he doing out here in the middle of nowhere in the middle of the night anyway? Was it the trees that seemed to be following him or maybe a courting couple or was it something else altogether?

He came to a clearing, a glade of some sort, lit up with an orange glow by the light from the very last rays of the sun which were beaming up towards the treetops. The magical light reminded him of the golden glow that came from the inside of a tabernacle where the priest kept the Holy Communion bread. It looked as if the glade had been carpeted with a layer of short mossy grass. Again, George felt that he was trespassing or that, somehow, he was treading on sacred ground. He couldn't quite explain it. There seemed to be no tall weeds or fallen branches or twigs. It looked as if someone had deliberately tidied the glade. He looked up, half expecting a glass dome of some kind but there were only the tall trees brushing the last rays of the lowering sun against the darkening sky where the brightest stars were already twinkling.

It was as if the glade had drawn him in, as if he couldn't help being there and wanting to stay there. It wasn't a good feeling nor was it a bad feeling. He felt it right that he should be there, fate or something or perhaps he felt, that he shouldn't be there at all. He strolled around the edge of the glade. A slight mound, also with a neat covering of grass, caught his eye. A bunch of wildflowers grew at one end of the mound. A shiver shot through his body and then a cold sweat overwhelmed him. Now the atmosphere changed, and he felt that he didn't want to be in this place after-all. The sun finally slipped below the horizon and a cold greyness closed around him.

Sobered somewhat by the sudden chill and the darkness, George left the glade and went through the woods and then he stood looking at Josh Cogan's meadow, correcting himself that it was no longer Josh Cogan's meadow and that time had passed. Time had indeed passed, and he could not expect things to be the same. He felt better now …. standing by the darkening meadow. What was it about the glade? Was it just his past? A silhouette stood out against the inky sky at one corner of the meadow …. "Well. I'll be …." He said aloud with a smile …. "*The Alamo* …. still standing …. impossible? Surely that old building should have caved in by now."

He gazed at the far-off shrine to his boyhood and walked along the darkening hedgerow towards it. His mind was full of thoughts of Pete and Alfie. Where are they now, he wondered. Grown men with wives and kids no doubt. Pete was certain to have loads of kids with his dirty little mind, he joked with himself. He remembered the puerile jokes they would eagerly tell one another and how they sniggered and laughed at the very mention of bums and other body parts.

As he went along the edge of the meadow, George felt a sudden sharp chill as if he had stepped into a freezer. He could have sworn that Alfie was standing there, blocking his way. A loud whisper came into his head. *Don't …. don't….* the second whisper fainter than the first. The warm summer night air returned as suddenly as it had left. The past returning, the *Alamo* and all that, he said to himself, the past playing tricks, trying to remind me of my age, trying to rub my nose in it because of Lisa. Well bollocks to all that, he thought. Tomorrow, I will be meeting the Contessa of Caqueux. He wondered what she might be like, probably a big sexy woman, just waiting for him to satisfy her, he smiled.

A gibbous moon had risen from the low clouds on the eastern horizon, bringing a silvery light to the land. The *Alamo* was there before him. He stood still, looking at the jagged walls, reaching up into the still night air. Surely, he thought, surely it can't still be there. Surely it can't still be standing after all these years. Even thirty odd years before, it was a wreck, a ruin, just crumbling walls. This old friend seemed to beckon him. As he moved forward, he tripped on a clump of weed which unbalanced him for a moment. He quickly regained his posture. His vision had grown with the encroaching darkness, allowing him to see the outlines of his surroundings. He went through the opening in the wall and then he was standing among the ruins of the *Alamo*.

It seemed to him to be as he had remembered it. But why had they not knocked it down? Surely it was ideal for some kind of development. His estate agent's mind was going through the possibilities, even that of buying the place himself.

He remembered the puerile spitting competitions he would have with his boyhood pals. Unable to resist, he made a mouthful of spit, threw his head forward and landed a great blob on the wall. Yep, he reckoned that would still beat anyone. The spit ran down the wall, quite visible against the old whitewash but then it seemed to darken, and a haunting thought struck him for the stream of spit seemed, for a moment, to resemble blood. A fear gripped him as he backed away from the wall and he felt a hot breath on the back of his head.

"Christ, who's there." George called out, jolting forward.

"Good evening and who might you be and what are you doing here at this time of night?"

George recognised the voice. "Oh, it's you Mr Thwaites."

"Ah, Mr Murray. It's a bit late in the day to be measuring."

George smiled. "Sorry, I was just out for a walk. I used to play here as a kid. I never thought this old place would still be here." He was wondering if Thwaites had seen him spitting against the wall.

"Strange to see anyone around here at such a time." Said Thwaites.

"Oh, I was just curious." Said George, relieved that it was probably too dark for Thwaites to see the puerile stream of spit running down the wall. "I do hope you don't mind my being here this late."

"No, not at all." Said Thwaites, shaking his head. "But it is dangerous here. It is only a matter of time before these old walls cave in. I was out with the dog, but I seem to have lost the brute. He's probably sinking his teeth into some poor little rabbit somewhere.

"Best be off then. Will I see you in the morning when I call on Miss Cavendish?" Said George.

"I'm afraid Miss Cavendish won't be there after all. She had to go away suddenly but don't worry, she'll be back tomorrow afternoon. I do hope we haven't messed you about."

"That's fine with me." Said George. "I have plenty of time, plenty of catching-up to do."

"You're staying in the village?"

"Yes. The Shamrock."

It seemed weird, two grown men having a conversation in an old rundown crumbling farm build, in a corner of a field under the moonlight. In another time, such a meeting might have been construed as being subversive.

"Well, I'd better be off." Said George as he stepped around Thwaites towards the opening in the wall.

"You can walk with me and cut through the meadow if you like. It will bring you onto the road and straight to the village .... Save you going back through the woods." Said Thwaites.

"Great." Said George, relieved that he wouldn't have to walk back through the woods in the dark, but he did wonder for a moment how Thwaites knew the route he had taken to get to *The Alamo*.

There was enough moonlight on the meadow to see a close face. Thwaites seemed a little more congenial now than he had when they first met. Sporadic animal shrieks came from the direction of the woods.

"Old Sammy must be after something." Said Thwaites.

A moment or so later, a panting noise rushed behind them. It was followed by some excited yapping and an enormous black figure of a dog charged past them as it thundered out of the long grass. The hound sprang about excitedly jumping at Thwaites.

"Ah, there you are, you old devil. What have you been up to? Found a nice rabbit for yourself?"

The big black dog was barely decipherable in the dark, but George felt its tail thrashing against his legs. Thwaites snapped his fingers, and the brute came to heel, whimpering like a lost puppy.

"What's the matter, Sammy." Said Thwaites. "Did you get a fright? Did you see something?"

Thwaites patted the dog as it continued whimpering.

"He's a big fella." Said George.

"Aye." Said Thwaites. He's alright if you feed him properly."

"I see." Said George. "He must have taken on something bigger than himself before he came thundering out of the dark woods."

"Or seen something." Said Thwaites. "Those woods are dangerous, especially at night."

He didn't say any more about the woods and George somehow sensed that the subject was closed. A corner of Caqueux House peeped out through the night.

"Care for a nightcap, before you go back to the Shamrock?" Said Thwaites.

Thwaites led George around to the rear of the main house where a farmyard building had been converted to a manager's house. Thwaites lived alone there. He led the way along a narrow stone walled passage and up a flight of timber stairs. A door at the top opened to a large lounge with a low timber beamed ceiling. Sammy followed them and took possession of a three-seat sofa, sprawling its length, defying anyone to move him. Whatever had scared the big brute had gone now and he was top dog again.

George could see Thwaites clearly now. Thwaites was wearing traditional country clothes, Cavalry Twill trousers, an open neck shirt with a well-worn tweed jacket with leather patches on the elbows and brown leather brogues with hefty soles. His face had reddened somewhat since they'd first met, probably the sun, George thought.

"What's your poison?" Said Thwaites.

"Anything at all. Drop of Paddy if you have it."

Thwaites opened a cabinet and selected a bottle of Paddy. He half-filled two whiskey tumblers and handed one to his guest. "Sláinte...... Cheers."

They sat on leather armchairs, facing each other, separated by a coffee table with the slumbering Sammy sprawled on his couch.

"Has the old place changed much since your childhood?" Said Thwaites.

George swallowed a gulp of the whiskey before answering.

"Well, I was never here in Caqueux House itself. I used to play, mostly in the meadow and along the old railway line, over by the lake of course and the old place where we met tonight, we used to call it *The Alamo*."

Thwaites chuckled. "Yes, I suppose it does look a bit like that."

"I'm amazed that it's still there."

"It's Madame. She won't knock anything like that. Says it's got character. She's a very stubborn woman but she pays the wages, so I don't argue."

Thwaites topped-up the glasses. Whether it was because of the drink, or the trip down memory lane or Lisa, a lightness came over George. Then he was seeing double, and Thwaites began to sound hypnotic.

"You know," said Thwaites, "it might be a good idea to postpone your meeting with her ladyship until the day after tomorrow. She'll be in a much better mood by then."

"That's fine with me." Said George. "As I said, I have plenty of time but perhaps I could come over in the morning and take some photos anyway."

"Sure." Said Thwaites. "You can work away."

* * *

Father Michael Casey checked his watch for the umpteenth time. Ten minutes to midnight. His nicotine-stained fingers stubbed out another cigarette-butt in the already full, cut-glass ashtray which he had balancing on the arm of his chair. Although he was only fifty-three years old, he looked ten years older. This was his eighth summer as parish priest of Ballynamarbh. Thinning grey hair, a gaunt face with an unhealthy complexion and dark shadows beneath his dark brown eyes were testament to his long war.

The Reverend Michael Casey was no ordinary priest. The stack of specialist books on the floor next to his armchair was proof of that. Since being ordained in his late twenties, he had travelled much of the Christian world investigating supernatural happenings. He had seen it all; ghosts, poltergeists, sightings, satanic rituals. He had seen it all or thought he had, until he was posted to Ballynamarbh. Until Ballynamarbh, most of what he had dealt with had some rational worldly explanation or he was able to deal with it through prayer and exorcism. Often, he would spend days alone in places whose crippling atmosphere would have petrified most mortals. Christ, prayer, the crucifix and holy water were his only weapons as he battled against the forces of evil.

Father Casey looked at the framed photographs on the sideboard. The faces of priests, who had served at Ballynamarbh, stared back; each one frozen in its own split second of time for all time. The weary face of Father Philpott stared out at him. Suspicions had grown with the death of Father Philpott. To the outside world, his death was a natural occurrence, a heart attack, struck down in his prime but the fears of a few older locals were related to the bishop; fears that an evil spirit or spirits were present in the village. Since Father Philpott's untimely death, other priests, who had served at Saint Vincent's, also died prematurely.

Michael Casey touched each picture, his thoughts trying to invoke, the souls of his dead predecessors. He took a bottle of whiskey from the sideboard and poured a shot which he swallowed in one gulp. He gasped as the whiskey shocked the muscles in his chest. He blessed himself and hung a rosary around his neck.

He left the room, switched off the light and crossed the narrow hall then stepped out into the garden. It was cooler than he'd expected. Part of the not quite full moon peered from behind a cloud. He gazed at it for a moment, wondering. A short walk along the garden path and across the small carpark led him to the side door of the church. Almost midnight, he thought. He slipped his right hand into a slit at the side of his cassock and found the key which he kept on a chain which hung from his belt. He opened the side door and slipped into the church. He had already left a light on there. He locked the door behind him and moved across the width of the church giving a respectful bow of his head as he passed in front of the altar. A few flames still flickered in the blobs of spent candlewax in the metal tray beneath the statue of the Virgin Mary. Father Casey took a fresh candle, holding its wick to one of the panicking flames while in his mind he prayed one more prayer.

A nerve grating noise ripped through the vaulted building as he pulled a prie-dieu some feet away from its usual position at the foot of the statue. He positioned the prie-dieu so that he could see all around him. Pulling his cassock up a few inches, Father Casey eased himself onto his knees.

He had gone through this ritual every midnight for the past month. He began his solitary vigil, checking his watch again. Twenty-five minutes after midnight. The old church was silent, quiet and eerie like the deceiving calm at the eye of a storm. His left hand gripped the Rosary as he anxiously rolled the beads between his fingers, and he concentrated on the words which were now a loud pleading whisper.

A vibration moved through the floor. It was just a rumble but enough to let him know that they had arrived. His whispered prayers became louder and now he was saying the words aloud. "Hail Mary full of grace, the lord is with thee ...." A noisy clamour echoed as if the main doors had been slammed shut by some force. The flames of the candles beneath the statue of the Virgin Mary fluttered as if a rogue breeze had disturbed them. Father Casey's prayers became more intense, his head raised, his eyes wide open, scanning, like a solo performer, into the darkness towards the back of a theatre. If anything appeared, he didn't want to miss it.

Another vibration shot through the floor, sending a shudder through his knees and the tips of his shoes which rested on the floor. He could feel them now. They were there in the pews close to him. Each night over the past week, the presence, whatever it was, had returned and each night it seemed to get stronger and bolder. The air around Father Casey was cold now, cold as ice, as if he were shut in a butcher's freezer. Then there came a moaning sound, somewhere above the altar. It grew louder for a while then fizzled out. They were close now, he thought, but still, he could see nothing. He felt sticky as the cold sweat made his shirt cling to his body. His head felt as if it had, somehow, become detached, the skin at the sides and the back of his head, tightening around his skull. Now, he could smell whatever it was that was invading this sacred place. He could feel it trying to torment him, taunting him, spying on him. A pungent choking stench filled the air as he prayed louder.

A voice, a foreign sounding man's voice, cried out from somewhere among the darkened pews .... "Sanctuaire .... sanctuaire".... A woeful, desperate pleading.

Another shuddering ripped through the floor. The pattern was the same as before but the intensity of the presence or whatever it was, had been increasing each night. And then, just like before, it receded again. It was over .... for another night at least.

He finished his prayers, blessing himself as the cries and the noises retreated and the air became still and warm again. His muscles ached like those of an old man as he pushed himself to a stand. He raised his head to look up at the face of the statue of the Virgin Mary and lit another candle, whispering a prayer of thanks that he had survived this latest onslaught. He pushed the prie-dieu back into its proper place in front of the statue and left the church, going back to his house to sleep safely in his warm bed.

Father Michael Casey had survived one more tussle with the unwanted visitors, but he knew that they would be back again the following night and after another few nights they would bring their macabre visitations to a climax. He poured himself another whiskey and lit another cigarette and his nerves calmed as he sat back in his armchair. It was only then that he noticed the violent rips and tears in his cassock.

* * *

The sleep shattering clatter of a diesel engine rattled up from the street below, pitching George out of his slumber and momentarily confusing him as to where he was and what day of the week it was. From his bed, he could see only the tops of tall trees against fluffy clouds as they sailed across the window frame of blue sky. The diesel engine revved up and the milk van, or whatever it was, moved away down the street, taking its annoying noise with it.

Lisa was still there, on his mind. It was as if she just wouldn't buzz off, but in truth George really didn't want her to buzz off despite his affirmations to the contrary. As he lay there, he couldn't remember how he got back to the hotel. He remembered his walk through the woods and the clearing with the enchanting light which suddenly vanished with the setting sun, but he had to think a bit to remember having a drink with Thwaites. George struggled with his thoughts. He remembered standing among the ruins of *The Alamo,* so eerie under the moonlight and his puerile spitting at the wall. Must lay off the booze, he told himself. With all that had happened over the past few days, he reckoned that it had all been taking its toll. He looked at his watch which was still on his wrist. He always took his watch off when he went to bed. It was after seven and he was surprised that he didn't feel hungover but suspected that it might sneak up during the day. Must get ready to visit the bold *Contessa,* he thought but then he remembered his conversation with Thwaites, that Miss Cavendish wasn't going to be there that morning. He settled back onto the pillow, pulling the warm duvet around him.

There were only a few people having breakfast in the dining room that morning. An elderly American couple, loudly planning their day and looking up the address of some poor, unsuspecting, long-lost cousins who probably never even knew that they had relatives living in New Jersey. A neat German couple, newlyweds perhaps, chatted away in harsh Teutonic tones. Probably discussing ways to make everything square, George mused. Lisa! His wishful thoughts fooled him for a moment as he spotted a similar looking lady through the glass doors to the hotel foyer. Stupid! He thought.

It was warm but cloudy when he went out onto the street. He sat into his car, having to carefully manoeuvre it from a tight space between two thoughtlessly parked cars. He drove down the street, under the old railway bridge where he had walked the night before, and out into the countryside.

Tyres screeched as George braked suddenly after realising that he had overshot the entrance to Caqueux House. He slipped the gear leaver into reverse and backed up the twenty yards or so. The gates were open, and the steering wheel spun willingly through his hands as he drove the car through the gates and along the short drive. The drive curled between trees and colourful blooming shrubs before opening into a wide gravelled sweep at the house. He parked behind Thwaites's blue Land Rover. Sammy strolled along as George stepped onto the gravel. The dog sniffed the tyres, cocked his leg, sniffed George's hand then looked around as if volunteering to give a guided tour. George didn't really like dogs but so long as they didn't bite him or slobber all over him then he was prepared to live and let live. He took his camera from the car boot and walked to the south side of the house, snapping as he went. The house seemed to be smaller than he had remembered or thought he had remembered. If it seemed smaller, then it had also changed from what it had been years before. The walls were painted with a light pink colour with French shutters on the windows. The tops of the half basement windows looked out across the lawn which was framed by a border of shrubs and flowers. A conservatory with a small indoor pool had been built onto one side. It could have been a country house, portrayed in a glossy magazine.

There was no sign of Thwaites. George wondered about what kind of car Emma Cavendish might drive, probably a sporty Italian job, he thought. Sammy was indeed a big brute, with a jet-black shiny coat. He followed George around as he looked for the most suitable angles to take good photographs.

The meadow was a green gold sea of long grass bowing gently in the light breeze.

"Stay boy. Stay." George commanded the dog as he headed in the direction of the *Alamo*. Sammy took no notice and followed George around the edge of the meadow. George hadn't been imagining things. The old ruin was indeed as he had remembered it. The jagged walls were still standing with clumps of weeds and small trees growing in the dirt floor. Sniffing around, Sammy seemed livelier now. At least his tail was wagging. George looked at the wall where he'd spat the night before. A silvery, snail-like streak ran down the cracked, weathered plaster. No blood, no vampires, no howling dogs. George smiled with a kind of relief, relief that he had been imagining things rather than having witnessed some bizarre occult happening. He raised his camera to his face and took a few photographs of the *Alamo*.

Sammy snarled at a particular spot in the middle of the *Alamo* and then he stood still for a moment. He snarled again, moving around that spot as if he had found something.

"What's the matter?" Said George. "Seen a rabbit or something?"

The dog turned his head to George, a sort of confused look on his face. He snarled again as if trying to talk.

"What's gotten into you, boy?"

Sammy let out a few barks then ran off into the meadow. George couldn't help wondering. Was his imagination playing up again? A shiver of fear shook through him, and he crossed himself as he hurried from the *Alamo* and out into the *safety* of the open meadow.

"Let's vamoose, pardner." He said, realising that the utterance had slipped out, not so much automatically but more …. well …. sort of spookily as if someone had switched on a recorder in his head or perhaps, he was reliving his boyhood games. He chuckled nervously as Pete and Alfie came into his mind. "Where are they now? What happened to them? He wondered.

There was still no sign of Thwaites at the house. George patted Sammy on the head, sat into his car and as he drove away, in his rear-view mirror, he could see the forlorn looking creature with a pathetic abandoned look, receding into the background.

George wanted to have the film developed as soon as possible so he drove into Polglas. He passed through Ballynamarbh, stopping to take a few photographs to use up the roll of film. The couples he had seen earlier at breakfast were getting into their cars outside the Hotel, the same cars that had been parked very close to George's car, making it difficult for him to drive out that morning. Bloody foreigners, he said to himself, bloody foreigners, immediately berating himself for letting Lisa's treachery warp his vision of the world, when hatred of one could lead to an irrational hatred of others. Bitch, he thought. Did he love her at that moment? He shrugged then fiddled with the radio buttons as he drove off, letting a smile form as he caught the lyrics of .... *and I say to myself* .... *what a wonderful world.*

George found a parking space close to the main street in Polglas. A film processing shop wasn't far away, where he left the roll of film, being assured that it would be ready by the early afternoon, giving him a few hours to kill. He was curious to see more of the places he knew as a boy and wanted to find out if anyone knew about or even remembered Alfie and Pete. He headed back to Ballynamarbh, went through the village, under the bridge and past Caqueux House for about a quarter of a mile or so. The narrow winding road was vaguely familiar in places. There was only one turn off to the left. He couldn't miss it. The triangular patch of grass at the junction was still there, a horse and cart traffic island. His memory was correct. The road narrowed to a hump-back bridge over the railway line. It narrowed a bit more, then swung to the left in a wide gritty sweep.

He stopped suddenly and there it was, the cottage where he had lived as a child. It all seemed so odd, being there after all these years. A lifetime had passed. The cottage seemed smaller than he'd remembered but there was no mistaking it. He remembered his mother, on her knees, scrubbing the doorstep, polishing the door knocker. The sweet smell of freshly cut grass made it all so real. It was as if he had stepped back in time. He happily remembered how he used to rake the grass whenever his father mowed the lawn and how he would make small haystacks. There was a picture somewhere, he thought, of him standing proudly, with a small garden fork, beside his neat stacks of grass. A great part of his past was there in front of him. But that was it, the past, another time, different people, some other George Murray.

A jet aeroplane whistled faintly high above as its vapour trail drew a straight white line across the blue sky, reminding George that it was a very different world now from when he was a boy. He slipped the gear lever into first and drove on.

A bit further along the same road, stood the cottage where Alfie lived. As he pulled up by a neat privet hedge, George could see the net curtains twitch a fraction. Another dog, a Jack Russell this time, darted along the garden path the moment when George put his hand on the gate. Vicious little teeth threatened as the Jack Russell yapped and snarled. Luckily, an old man appeared at the front door, shouting at the dog to stop, but it just kept on barking excitedly or threatening, George wasn't quite sure which. The old man, his sleeves rolled up, wearing braces and leaning on a walking stick, hobbled towards George and the dog.

"He won't harm you." Said the old man, brushing the dog away with his walking stick. "Come on in boy."

"Hello." Said George, his hand outstretched.

"Nice day." Said the old boy as he groaned his worn old body onto a garden seat. "Take the weight off your feet, boy."

George sat on the garden seat. The old man could well have been Alfie's father.

"Mr Dawes, right?"

The old man nodded. "I am Indeed but …. you have me now boy?"

"Ah, you wouldn't remember me. I was at school with Alfie."

The old man said nothing for a moment. He just stared at the ground with both hands resting on the crook of his stick. After a few moments, he looked up. A troubled countenance had come across his face and his eyes were tearful.

"My lad passed away …. 'tis nearly seven years now."

"Oh." Said George. "I didn't know. I am so sorry." He went silent, feeling as if he had just punched the poor man in the face.

"Ah, sure you weren't to know, boy."

"Can I ask what happened?"

"It was God's will. That's all." Said the old man. His voice and demeanour were full of sadness.

It was obvious that the old man didn't want to talk about it and George tried to change the subject, but the damage had been done and this sadness was a permanent part of his life anyway.

"He's over in St Vincent's, alongside his mother. God rest them."

There was nothing George could do now. He wanted to leave quickly but that would have seemed rude, so he just sat there, alongside the old man, on the garden bench for a little while and they talked about Ballynamarbh and how it had changed or not changed over the years. A little time passed then George went back to his car and left the poor old guy with his thoughts and his memories, his sadness and his God.

As he drove, George was thinking about Alfie and how strange life could be. A kid he knew for just a short while in his early life. It might as well have been some other person, in some other place, some other world. St Vincent's church loomed in the distance, as he drove towards Ballynamarbh. He was in two minds as to whether he should visit Alfie's grave. *Ah .... sure .... might as well ....* he thought as he pulled over by the church.

A couple of magpies pecked at the ground around the old headstones. George was thinking about the old saying .... one for sorrow, two for joy .... *Well, that's that theory gone out of the window,* he said to himself. A path led along the side of the church to the newer burial ground, the old churchyard having become fully occupied a few years before. The warmth and light from the sun was stronger here but there was also a feeling of loneliness and melancholy as if the dead here were not yet at complete rest, as if they were still around in some way. Here lay the remains of people who were still with the living, still remembered, their voices, their laughter and their crying too, all still resonating in the hearts and minds of people who knew them. The headstones were newer, white and grey, stone and marble, all standing upright, unlike the older churchyard where the headstones were looking as if they themselves had given up with the passing of time and were keeling over with the weight of the years, of the decades and of the centuries.

A manicured path guided George through the neat rows of headstones. His eyes scanned as he went among the well-kept graves and family plots, stopping from time to time to read the inscriptions on the headstones …. a beloved mother …. taken from us …. a loving father …. R.I.P ….

A fresh bunch of flowers caught George's eye …. There it was: *Alfred Patrick Dawes.* George stood still, not knowing quite what to do with his hands as he read the chiselled lettering on the stone. In one sense he felt nothing for the man buried six feet beneath him. After all, he didn't really know him, another lifetime, another George, another Alfie. He never knew the teenager, the man, the adult. In another sense George felt a deep affinity with Alfie. He could see clearly, the face of the boy he once knew. It was the face of the kid he had played with, joked with, fought with. The thought crossed his mind that it could have been he, himself who might have died so young, so prematurely. What if someone had said to the three boys playing in the *Alamo* all those years ago that one of them would be dead before they reached forty-five? George's mind often conjured such tormenting thoughts. He felt that he should say something to his childhood friend. He spoke aloud.

"Well, me aul pal. I didn't know. I hope that wherever you are, you are happy. I've been thinking of you and our old pal Pete, quite a bit lately…….."

There was no mention on the stone about a wife or children, just Alfie's name and the dates of his birth and death. How short life was, he thought, as his own mortality came to his mind. Better make the most of it while I can, he thought as he walked away from Alfie's grave.

Father Casey was arranging leaflets on the noticeboard in the church porch. He looked up as George passed.

"Nice day." He said, nodding at George.

"Hello Father." Said George as he stepped closer to the Priest. "Tell me Father, have you been here long?"

Father Casey gazed for a moment, his eyes tired and bloodshot after his ordeal of the night before. "Ah, a few years now."

"Did you know Father Philpott?" Said George.

Father Casey's stare became more intent. "You knew him?"

"Yes." George smiled. "He used to hear my confessions when I was a child."

Father Casey continued pinning leaflets to the noticeboard.

"Tell me Father. I was looking at a grave in the new part of the cemetery …. I don't suppose that you would have known a man by the name of Alfie Dawes?"

The priest stopped what he was doing and turned to George.

"You knew him …. too?"

"Yes. We played together. My family moved to Dublin after primary school, and I never heard of him again. I didn't know that he had passed away, until today. I don't suppose you know what happened to him?"

The priest thought for a moment. "Ah sure it was a tragedy by all accounts. The poor boy just lost his way, one bad thing after another."

"Did he take his own life?"

"It was God's will." Said Father Casey, not really wanting to acknowledge that people actually ended their own lives.

George stood with his hands in his pockets, pensively circling the sole of his right shoe over a patch of dusty bald earth. "I'd really like to know what happened to him, Father."

"It is better to leave the dead to their rest. Now if you'll excuse me, I have calls to make. Good day to you." Said Father Casey as he pushed the heavy door open and went into the church.

George went back to his car, somewhat confused by this brush-off. Why didn't the priest want to talk about it? Surely the Catholic Church was enlightened enough to admit that people did take their own lives.

He ate a light lunch of sandwiches with tea at a café in Polglas. His mind was jumping about, switching between Lisa and Alfie. Suicide? Jesus, he thought, remembering the time when he was close to it himself. A woman was involved then too. How strange and self-destructive was the state his mind got itself into. He had given all his love and self to that woman and then she suddenly went and broke it all off. He remembered how lonely and how inadequate he felt. How reclusive he became, neglecting his job and his health. How, for months he simply could not face the world, afraid that he might bump into her when she was with someone else. *How cruel love could be,* he thought. He remembered the day when he took a rope from the boot of his car. He was sober, stone-cold sober; his mind as clear about what he was doing as it had ever been and that was probably the most frightening aspect about it all, cold calculating suicide as if his mind had come to the logical conclusion that death was the only way out. After that there would be no pain, just silence and nothingness. Early in the morning, four o'clock, it was, George remembered. The wee hours as they say, when deep emotions can mess you about even more. He remembered how quiet it was, so early, so dark, so still. He could slip out of the world when everyone else was asleep. How vividly it stayed in his mind ever since. He remembered sitting on the stairs drawing the rope through his hands. The feel of the rope seemed to be in tune with his hopelessness. Then he made a noose and even now, he could still see himself as he looked up to see where he might hang it.

Now, as George thought of those terrible dark days, he felt so lucky that, either it hadn't been his time or that he was just plain coward. Either way, he thanked his lucky stars that he hadn't gone through with it and that he was still in the land of the living, unlike poor old Alfie who was now six feet under.

As he ate his lunch in the café in Polglas, he noticed a good-looking blonde woman giving him the eye. He smiled back then looked away. He didn't want anyone else in his life right now. He finished his lunch and went to look around Polglas. As he followed the disused tram tracks along the waterfront, he remembered talk by older people about the old trams that once served Polglas and their nostalgia for the last tram as it went along the main street and down to the quays, terminating beyond the town's park. Now, even the green double-decker bus had had its day, replaced mostly by a single deck small fleet in bright colours, convenient urban transport.

"Not quite ready yet." Said the young woman behind the counter at the film developing shop. "About five minutes."

"Fine. I'll wait." Said George as he began to pace the floor.

The five minutes was, of course, ten but eventually the latest batch of developed snaps were sent through. A quick glimpse at the first few photographs and George was happy that he had been given the right ones. He tucked the wallet of photographs into his jacket pocket, paid the lady and left.

Mid-afternoon, and the pedestrianised main street was heaving with people. Casual clothes, T-shirts, jeans and trainers seemed to be the order of the day. It used to be almost a *criminal offence*, George remembered, to be seen downtown in anything other than your Sunday best or school uniform. Tourists window-shopped among the locals and people sat in the shade of trees on long benches. George sat at the end of a bench and looked through the photographs. The first few were of Caqueux House itself. Sammy seemed to have wangled his way into one of them. Then the meadow with its golden colours; perfectly portrayed. George was pleased with his photography skills.

A particular photograph caught his attention. Surely a mistake! *They have given me someone else's photograph.* He thought, at first glance. He looked again. A *child at play? Not mine,* he thought, and he continued thumbing through the wad of pristine shiny photographs some of which were of Caqueux and some of which were photographs he had taken over the previous few weeks in Dublin. He recognised all of them except for the one of a child at play. He was certain that it was not his. There were a few children on the periphery of his life, and he always kept his distance from friends with children. Anyway, he only ever used that particular camera for his work.

He flicked through the photographs again, returning to the rogue picture. He studied it as he sat on the bench amidst the people on the Main Street. A puzzled frown came over his face.

George stared at the colour photograph; a child, a little boy playing, naked from the waist up, a skinny kid posing as some sort of tribal native. He couldn't quite make out the detail of the scene or the face. He felt in his jacket pocket for his reading glasses, cursing himself for either leaving them in the car or in his room back at the Shamrock. Puzzled by the photograph, he slipped it back into its wallet with the wad of photographs and went back to his car.

An annoying drizzly rain was settling on his windscreen as he sat into the car. George started the engine and turned on the wipers and the demister. His reading glasses were there in the glove box. The picture of the little boy was quite clear now. George was amazed, thinking intently as the wipers slid back and forth across the windscreen with their own irritating whining lament. The old walls of the *Alamo* showed vivid and there, in the opening, through which he had so often run, stood a little boy wearing old fashioned short pants and sandals. Couldn't be? He thought. Couldn't possibly be Alfie? He studied the face. Was time playing tricks? This must surely be some kind of coincidence, or was he going mad? He thought he could remember what Alfie and Pete looked like, how their faces were but of course he couldn't be sure.

He kept looking at the face. Alfie had ginger hair. This kid seemed to have reddish hair too. He remembered how they used to strip to the waist, daubing streaks of mud across their chests, like Red Indians. He thought of going back to the film shop but decided against it for fear that they might think he was nuts.

He threw the wallet of pictures on the passenger seat beside him, flicked the indicator leaver on the steering column and pulled out into the traffic. The drizzle was sheeting heavily now as low clouds moved in from the coast giving a slippery wet surface to the road. George was wondering if he might be losing his mind. Maybe it was not only Lisa that was getting to him but work also might be having an adverse effect. He wondered, too, about this sudden bout of nostalgia. Was this a part of his psyche, wanting to retreat to the safety and carefree days of his childhood or was something else taking him back? *Should see a doctor,* he thought. *Need a good rest. Maybe quit altogether and buzz off to Australia or somewhere. Start a new life.*

Ballynamarbh was grey and dull when it rained. A few people, dashed about beneath umbrellas while rivulets of rain ran down the main street towards the bridge. George parked near to the Shamrock Hotel. He remained in the car for a few minutes. He was deep in thought, and he didn't really relish the idea of getting wet. When he had enough of sitting there with the windows fogging up, he hurried out of the car and made a dash for the hotel.

Feeling tired and more than a little confused, George threw the wad of photographs on the floor beside the bed. It was comforting to lay there in the warmth after the rain but now Alfie was on his mind, as was Alfie's father, the grave and the priest and not least, the strange photograph. Still, it was a relief from constantly thinking about Lisa but as he thought that thought, she was back on his mind again. He reached to the floor beside the bed for the wallet of photographs. The pictures seemed clearer now as he examined them under the bedside lamp but …. but where was the picture of the little boy who appeared playing cowboys and Indians. He flicked frantically through the wad of photographs, but that particular photograph wasn't there. He singled out the one that showed the *Alamo* but there was definitely no little boy there now. Frustrated with himself and the whole damn thing, he threw the photographs back onto the floor, took off the rest of his clothes, slipped under the duvet and shut the world out.

The fine weather had returned when he woke. The afternoon had gone and now it was early evening. He looked through the photographs again as he lay propped up against two fat pillows. There was no sign of a little boy or any children in any of them. George yawned, rubbing his eyes. Must have that check-up, he told himself, first thing when I get back to Dublin, but he wasn't sure in his heart that that was the problem. He was certain that he did see a boy in one of the photographs but right then it was easier to dismiss it.

A warm shower made him feel much better. He dressed in jeans and a sweater then stood in front of a mirror and studied his own face. His eyes were bloodshot and tired, appearing sunk in their recesses above dark unhealthy rings. His skin looked blotchy and pale. Maybe it was the light over the mirror; a cruel sort of white light that never did anyone any favours. No, it wasn't the light, he admitted, or half admitted. He felt his age, he felt older. He forced a smile, attempting to quell the rebellion before him in the mirror.

George searched through the phonebook at the reception desk. Murphy …. Murphy …. Murphy. His finger sped down the columns of Murphys. Murphy, probably the most common name in Ireland. A longshot, George thought that since Alfie's people were still in the area and so Pete's people might still be here too. When he had scanned all the Murphys, he gave up. No Peter Murphys ….. and he didn't know what Pete's father's first name was. George went into the restaurant and dined alone.

As he sat at the bar afterwards, George thought the old codger at the end of the bar might just know about the Murphys. Eager as ever for a free pint, the old codger soon began volunteering information.

"Would they be the same Murphy's that used to have the piggery over at Finn's Cross?" Said the old codger.

George thought for a moment. "Yes, I think you're right. They were pig farmers, but I don't remember Finn's Cross."

"Ah, sure they've all gone, 'tis twenty years now, I'd say. The bank took it off 'em." Said the old codger, his nicotine-stained fingers bringing the last of his cigarette to his lips.

"Any idea of what became of the sons?" Said George.

The old codger stubbed out his cigarette-butt in the ashtray while fans of pale white smoke flared from his nostrils.

"Let me think now …. Yes, three of 'em went off to America and one went for the priesthood. The last fella, I think."

"Pete was the youngest." Said George. "But the priesthood? I would never have thought that Pete was cut out for the priesthood …. a wild little devil. But then I only ever knew him as a kid and then for only about three years at the most.

"Sure, the Almighty, he works in mysterious ways." Said the old codger, with an earthly sort of wisdom. "And how often do you see a quiet young fella turn out to be an awful blaggard altogether and a young garsún who's a right little fecker, turning out to be a saint?" He smiled as if he was the font of all knowledge.

"True enough." Said George. "Do you know where he went or where he is now?"

The old codger took another gulp of his pint. "He's only a few miles away from this very spot as far as I know. I think he's over in St Kevin's."

George thought for a moment. "You mean the mental hospital?"

"That's right, boy. He takes care of the sick, a real vocation."

Loud music played, drowning out the conversation. The old codger and George looked around. A couple of guitar players had taken positions by the inglenook fireplace; a music session for the rest of the evening.

"For the tourists." Said the old codger, leaning towards George's ear. He placed his empty glass on the counter with more than a little ceremony. George got the message and he and the old codger settled into a nice drinking session. The music, the chat and the crack were good, and George was mildly drunk as he went to bed.

George slept a good sleep but awoke suddenly. Fully alert, his mind was racing as his eyes gazed at the ceiling above the bed. Again, he had forgotten to remove his watch from his wrist before he went to sleep. The furniture in the room languished ghostly under an eerie dawn light. For a moment, George thought that it was still the evening before. He lifted his left arm, angling his wrist to catch the dull light on the face of his watch. Need a drink, he thought, need water. George left the bed. Yawning and scratching, he looked out through the window. The hotel gardens below were silent and still coated in the cool night air with flowers waiting to open with the sun's first warming rays. He had a clear view up towards St Vincent's church as it loomed over the village, seeming to stand there forever, a guardian of rural morality. A few headstones peeped above the wall surrounding the church.

George's warm alcoholic breath misted on a patch of the window, and he wiped the condensation away with the tips of his fingers. Another yawn forced its way over his jaws as he rubbed his eyes, trying to see clearly some grey figure that seemed to move about among the headstones. The figure stood still for a short while and George thought that it was looking down at him. Then it was gone. George could have sworn that it had vanished just like a ghost. But he couldn't be sure. He tried to rationalise what he had seen or thought he had seen in the grey dawn light. He had drink taken and was suffering from a broken heart. *No*! He shouted at himself, his loud spontaneous utterance raping the tranquillity of his room. Definitely not a broken heart! Women! Who needs them anyway?

The same tourists were in the breakfast room as had been the morning before, the Germans at their designated table, the Americans at theirs and a few new people were there too. It was after nine when George phoned Emma Cavendish to arrange a time for his visit. "I'm here all day." She said. "Probably, I'll be down by the lake if it's this morning."

* * *

Wet patches of road hid beneath the tree shadows as he drove towards Caqueux. A deep blue sky topped the landscape, and the air was fresh after some overnight showers. George was wondering what the famous Emma Cavendish would look like. Her voice over the phone was certainly sexy, measured with a very slight vulnerable tone. *Perhaps, perhaps* …. He thought. He thought of Lisa again. *Well, she's been screwing around so I can too*. He said to himself. *Oh, forget her!* …… *Forget her!*

He checked his face in the driver's mirror as he pulled up on the sweep of gravel at the front of Caqueux House. No Land Rover, he noticed. *Thwaites must be out or away …. all the better for chatting up the Miss Cavendish*. He thought. A yellow Mercedes Coupé sat beneath the overhanging branches of a rhododendron tree. No Sammy either. Perhaps he had eaten old Thwaites. George smiled.

He went around to the side of the house. A sliding glass door had been left partly open, so he pushed it back further and he stepped inside. The conservatory housed a swimming pool, not a very big one but large enough, with an array of wicker sun lounge chairs. The water shimmered invitingly, beneath the glass. Another door seemed to lead into the house itself. This one was closed. There was a bell on the frame. George rang the bell. Nervously, he stepped back and looked around while anticipating a response. Nobody came. He rang again then paced by the pool for a while. Again, no one came so he went back outside, looking around for a short while before heading off for the lake.

The path took him to the *Alamo* and then through the woods. He passed through the glade where he had been two nights before. Wildflowers gave an air of theatre to the glade, as if waiting for a troupe of dancers to enter. Momentarily George looked at mound. He wondered. A shiver shot through him as if someone had walked on his grave, and he hurried his step.

He climbed the railway embankment and stood at the top where the trains once clattered along but had since been returned to rural tranquillity. The small lake glistened silvery in the morning sun, momentarily blinding him. A cluster of trees encroached onto the stony beach, a few hundred yards in the distance. He could see what looked like a rowing punt and something colourful shimmering in the morning sun.

George walked along the old rail track towards the cluster of trees. The sun warmed his face and his shoulders, making him take his jacket off and carry it, finger-hooked, over his shoulder. The track veered off to the left and a path to the right sloped down through weeds and scrub towards the trees on the beach.

A hammock, slung between two trees, bulged slightly as its occupant shifted to look up.

"Miss Cavendish?" Said George, stopping himself from saying *I Presume,* for fear of sounding corny.

The woman sat up and eased herself out of the hammock. "Tricky things to get in and out of. You must be Mr Murray but please call me Emma."

George extended his arm, trying not to stare too much at this beautiful woman wearing a black swimming suit. She took a wrap from the hammock and with a catwalk flourish, she tied it around her waist to make a skirt.

"Welcome to my desert island." She said.

"It certainly looks like one, tranquil and private." He said, then paused for a moment. "Have we met before?" George was sifting through his memory.

"Perhaps." She said with a teasing grin.

She was, George guessed, about fifty, fifty-five at most Whatever age she was, she looked great. Her hair was long and dark, and her movements were graceful and nun-like.

"Would you be so kind as to tie the boat?" She said as if she was used to having servants around her.

George felt like telling her to go jump in the lake, but business is business. Obediently, he tied the rowing boat to a stake in the ground. "Been out on the lake?" He said.

"Yes, whenever I'm here. Always go for a row in the morning." She said.

She gathered her belongings into a canvass shoulder bag, pulled her sunglasses from their perch above her forehead and slipped her feet into a pair of yellow flip-flops.

"Shall we talk as we go along?" She said.

A stumble on the uneven stony shore led her to fall against George who quickly caught her arm, feeling her soft flesh while at the same time getting a whiff of her perfume or was it sun-tan oil? He wasn't quite sure. Either way, it was nice.

"Dangerous around here if you're not careful." He said.

"Danger is living." Emma Said, philosophically and smiled as a light breeze whipped a few strands of hair across her face.

They climbed the embankment, crossed the old railway line, went down the other side of the embankment and took the path through the woods.

"Arthur tells me you know this area." She said.

George thought for a moment, realising that she was referring to Thwaites. "Well, a little. I lived around here as a child, many moons ago."

Her womanly curves seemed to slink through the air as she led the way. She stopped when they reached the glade.

"Delightful little place. Don't you think." She said.

"Enchanting but is that a grave over there?" Said George.

"They say that it is." She said. "It is supposed to be that of a Gipsy. From time to time, a bunch of flowers are left there but no one knows who does it.

"A haunting place." Said George.

"It is, isn't it." Emma's voice had turned to a whisper as if she were in tune with the glade.

They were facing each other now as they stood almost in the centre of the glade. Her eyes seemed to enchant. To George, at that moment, she could have been an angel with all the womanly beauty of the world rolled into one. He deliberately broke his gaze and continued towards the far side of the glade and the way through the trees towards the meadow.

"Might as well see the old farm building while we're passing. Only a pile of old stones really, but it might have an influence on your valuation." Said Emma.

George nodded but he didn't mention the fact that he knew the old building from long ago. A gentle fragrance trailed Emma as they walked. Then they were at the *Alamo*. Déjà vu was the phrase that came to George's mind. Emma turned to face him and all he could do was to stare. He could not explain it, not to himself, not to anyone. A kind of karmic resonance fuzzed his head as she stood before him and then he remembered the Tinker girl.

Over the past few days, he had thought about Alfie and Pete and their play and school and the things they used to get up to, but he had forgotten all about the Tinker girl who came to Ballynamarbh that last summer. Her haunting words came back to him. "Beware the blue moon."

"Are you ok?" Said Emma. "You seem a little shaken."

"No, I'm fine. It must be the rich country air down here. Not used to it. So how many acres in all?" He said trying to sound as if he was with it.

"About three hundred. Mostly good land. The majority has been let out." She said.

They left the *Alamo* and went back along by the meadow towards Caqueux.

"Have you thought of a value, yourself?" George said.

"No, not really."

"That's my job. Right!" Said George.

"Of course."

George was thinking that she was ok and that talk of her being a stuck-up old bitch was just that. Emma Cavendish seemed to be quite a nice woman, but he reminded himself that he should not jump to conclusions until he knew her.

"Have you an ordnance map of the property?" He said.

"There is one somewhere. Pity Arthur is away. He knows where all these things are." She said with a slight little girl lost look as if it suited her, at that particular moment, to portray a girlish innocence.

When they reached the garden at Caqueux house, George took his tape measure and a clipboard from the boot of his car, and he followed Emma through the conservatory and into the house.

"You'll have to excuse me while I go and put some clothes on." Said Emma, leaving George standing in the hall as she went upstairs. There was little evidence of modernisation.

In fact, it all looked quite Victorian. The walls were decorated with floral patterns. Polished red and cream tiles covered the hall floor. Dark-wood doors led off to the reception rooms, to the kitchen and to the basement, while dark-wood banisters stepped invitingly up the red-carpeted stairs.

George stepped into one of the reception rooms which turned out to be the lounge. Warm bright sunshine spilled through two large windows which looked out over the garden towards the meadow. He took a half turn to face the fireplace and was taken aback by what he saw. Everything in the room was eclipsed by the picture that hung on the wall.

"You have seen it before." He heard Emma's voice.

He turned towards her. She was standing in the doorway, a mischievous grin on her face. He turned again towards the picture.

"So, you were the woman at our auction. I knew I had seen you before."

They stood there looking at the painting for a moment.

"Quite at home here, isn't it?" She said with a certain amount of glee.

"It certainly is. But I am curious. Why is it so important to you?"

Emma shrugged. "No particular reason that I can say. I knew that I just had to have it. The auctioneer helped as well." She smiled again.

"It looks as if it was created especially for this room." He said. "Magnificent! …. Fits in perfectly. You have an eye for art,"

"I like to think so." She smiled.

George smiled back. "I'd better take some details." He said changing the subject.

Emma held the end of the tape as he measured each room. An ancient black range, set into its alcove, dominated the kitchen. Everywhere was spotlessly clean but old fashioned. It was like stepping into some rural museum or perhaps he had somehow stepped back into the past.

Emma led the way up the stairs. The first-floor layout was similar to that of the ground floor. George followed her into the main bedroom.

"Different. Don't you think?" She said.

George was looking around the room. "It has its attraction." He was being diplomatic. "It's quite …. "

"Romany." She said before he could finish his sentence. "Intriguing people, Gipsies, don't you think?"

"I wouldn't know. I never had much to do with them." He said with a shrug as he made more notes.

"Haven't you?" She said with a kind of rhetorical tone in her voice. Her eyes pierced him, giving him that light, nebulous feeling again. "I have preserved much of this house just as it was when I first came here. The old place has a certain feeling to it. It would be like going against nature to change it. The only concessions I have made to modernity are the conservatory and the swimming pool."

"How long have you been here?" Said George.

Emma gazed though the window out over the lush green countryside, pretending that she hadn't heard the question or at least ignoring it. After a little while she turned to him. Her come to bed eyes; deep and all consuming, as if daring him to make a move. George stared back, thinking that if he made a move then it would be when he was good and ready. It was as if she was able to read his mind. She turned away to resume her gaze on the countryside.

The bathroom was no surprise. It was as archaic as the rest of the house with light green tiles all around to about shoulder height with white panelling above. An elegant cast iron bath sat by a frosted window.

"Room enough for two in that." Said George, immediately regretting the innuendo.

"Indeed. It really is quite comfortable." She said.

They went downstairs, George kept adding to his notes. "What about the basement?"

"Oh, I nearly forgot." She said stepping towards the basement door.

A mouldy, damp odour wafted from the half dark stairwell as she opened the door.

"There's a light switch there somewhere." She said as if giving orders again.

George swept his hand along the wall until he felt the switch. A dull yellow light came on below, showing the bottom few dusty steps and the stone floor below.

"Is it safe?" He said, jokingly, as he cautiously took the first step down towards the stone floor below. The damp, mouldy smell was worse now. At the bottom of the stairs there was a large open area with sturdy wood beams supporting the floor above. Daylight struggled through the windows which were partly above ground level and partly below. Three doors led to separate rooms.

"Hasn't been used much, has it." Said George, as he turned around to find himself speaking to the musty air. Emma wasn't there. He tried the handles of the closed doors, but they were all locked. He turned and Emma was there again. Startled, he gave a slight shudder.

"Oh, I thought you had gone back upstairs." He said.

Emma seemed different now, as if observing him or trying to unnerve him, he couldn't quite put his finger on it. He could smell her perfume again, subtly overwhelming the damp air.

"Servants quarters." She said.

Something triggered in his memory when she said that. He remembered old Josh Cogan's housekeeper who hanged herself in the *Alamo*. A shiver went through his body as if someone had just walked on his grave.

Emma didn't have the keys to those basement rooms so George took whatever notes he could, and they went back up the mouldy stairs into the colourful, warming daylight.

"Tea?" She said.

"Yes. That would be nice."

He relaxed in one of the wicker chairs by the swimming pool while Emma went to make tea. She returned a few minutes later carrying a tray with an exotic teapot with equally exotic, bright green teacups on saucers.

"It's herbal tea, my own special blend. I hope you like it."

"I'll try anything once."

Emma poured the tea with a flourish as if she were performing in a drama. Their eyes met again as she handed a cup on a saucer to George. He paused before he put his lips to it. It had an odd taste; sweet, aging but somehow comforting.

"Very nice." He said, nodding.

"It will ease away aches and pains. Good for the nerves too."

"Do I look nervy then?" Said George.

George was puzzled by the fact that she didn't seem to want to talk business. After all that was why he was there. She posed as she sipped from her bright green teacup. It was as if she was trying to entice or seduce him.

"Are you in a hurry back to Dublin?" She asked.

"No, not really. I thought I might take a few days rest while I am around here."

Emma smiled. "So why don't you come over this evening? I'll be down by the lake. I'll be all alone, just me and the stars."

George was hesitating, wondering.

"Do come. It's lovely there at this time of year. We might even see a shooting star …. More tea?"

Emma filled his cup and as he sipped, a strange feeling came over him. It wasn't a bad feeling but more of a deep relaxation, as if he was watching and thinking in slow motion.

"Well, I should be going." Said George. "I have to make another visit and I must make some phone calls."

"Until later then." Said Emma who remained seated as George got to his feet.

* * *

The clock on the dashboard read two thirty. George checked it against his wristwatch. He rubbed his face, wondering where all the time had gone. He thought it might only have been about midday. Surely …. he thought, surely …. he couldn't have lost track of time to that extent. Maybe Emma Cavendish really was a witch? Maybe that tea was a drug? Stupid, he thought …. stupid …. on with the day.

Passing back through Ballynamarbh, he took the road west. Often, he liked to test his car near to its limits but right then he was content to just motor along at his ease and enjoy the trip. He saw the signpost for St Kevin's Hospital. He indicated, turned left and drove along a minor road for about a mile and then he was driving through the tall gates of St Kevin's.

A black car came towards him as he drove along the single-track drive which led to the hospital, forcing him to pull into a passing place. It was shining black hearse. Its polished chrome and windows all glinted in the sun. George blessed himself as it drew level with his car, his eyes fixing on the light brown coffin, eerily modelling itself in its glass display. It was like a pointing finger, reminding him of his own mortality. Something pathetic about a hearse laden with a coffin and travelling alone, he thought ….. Lonely, without a funeral cortege.

St Kevin's was an old redbrick Victorian edifice, grim and forbidding, a barracks of a building with rows of narrow mournful windows as if it were a long waiting room to sorrow. George parked next to some other cars at the front of the building, overlooking a panorama of Irish countryside, the only redeeming feature of the whole place. He went up the steps to the main entrance. A push with his hand had no effect so he reached for the white thumb-bell on its brass mounting. He could hear the ringing resonating like a loud sting on the other side of the door. Waiting, he turned to look at the view of the wide sweep of parkland, dotted with elegant leafy trees. After a civilised wait, he pressed the bell again. Then a clump and a click and the door opened.

"Hello." Said the little nun who stood there wearing the traditional black habit, black veil and a white stiffened wimple, all set off by the crucifix to which she devoted her life.

"Hello Sister." Said George. "I believe you have a Father Murphy working here. Would it be possible to see him?"

The little nun thought for a moment. "You'd better come in."

George stepped inside and she closed the big wooden door behind him.

"Would you wait here please?" She said in an efficient nun-like manner.

He nodded. "Thank you, Sister."

She turned and walked, like an elegant breeze, to the far end of the long entrance hall where she went into what George presumed to be an office. George looked around, thinking what an austere place it was, and all watched over by a statue of the Virgin Mary which stood elevated on a plinth in an alcove. He studied the statue, the hands forever joined in prayer and the angelic face that gazed down on the world. It reminded him of his school days when the class said prayers. Often, as a child, he would secretly laugh at this twice daily ritual when the prayers were in full swing. It all sounded like some strange communal mumble with few, if any, of his fellow pupils understanding the words. George certainly had trouble saying the words and remembered how he would make up his own secret, childish version .... *Hail Mary not full of grace. The lord is not with thee* .... A mischievous grin came to his face as he thought of his own child's mind.

George's face straightened quickly as the office door opened. The same little nun came out and came towards him.

"Mother Antonia will be with you shortly, if you don't mind waiting a little longer."

"Not at all, Sister. Thank you."

The little nun bowed her head slightly, turned and went up the wide staircase, moving as if making a noise would be some kind of violation or simply bad manners. Whatever it was, George liked it, feeling good with the knowledge that there were people around who were not noisy or vulgar.

A few minutes passed before the office door opened again. A taller nun, peering over half-moon glasses approached.

"Hello, I'm Mother Antonia, the Mother Superior here."

George introduced himself.

"I'm looking for Father Peter Murphy. I understand he is stationed here."

A hint of a smile came to her face. "I think you have it wrong, Mr Murray." She said as she slid her hands together, making them disappear into the wide cuffs of each opposite sleeve.

"I don't follow." Said George.

"Well, we do have a Father Peter Murphy here alright, but he is a patient."

George was surprised but not surprised. "I'm only going on second-hand information. So, tell me, Reverend Mother, would he be about my age?"

"Yes." She nodded.

"Can I meet this man? I am guessing that he is the man I am looking for. We were at school together, just down the road at Ballynamarbh." Said George, motioning his hand in the vague direction of the village. I left Ballynamarbh with my parents years ago. I thought that since I was in the area this week, I might look him up. I was told that he had joined the priesthood and that he was working here."

"I see." Said Mother Antonia. "Perhaps I should tell you."

They walked to the end of the entrance hall and Mother Antonia motioned him into her office. The sun shone into the room, giving it a much warmer atmosphere than the gloomy entrance hall. Mother Antonia sat at her mahogany desk and George sat into a leather armchair. The Mother Superior leaned slightly forward in her seat. She spoke slowly.

"This is quite unethical, but I am going to take you into my confidence. So, whatever I tell you, I trust that you will respect the situation."

"Of course, Reverend Mother. I do understand." Said George.

Mother Antonia sighed. "Well, Father Pete as we call him was admitted into St Kevin's about eight years ago. Prior to that he had been in Africa for a few years and returned to take up parish work in Ballynamarbh. It seems that he suffered a mental breakdown, but we just don't know why. He was perfectly happy, according to all reports. Something seems to have snapped in his mind, shattering his life. We do know about breakdowns and many people respond to therapy and love. But in poor Father Pete's case, we just cannot get through to him."

"Are we talking about the same person?" Said George. "After all it has been a lifetime since we have laid eyes on each other."

Mother Antonia thought for a moment. "Does the name Alfie mean anything to you?"

George's eyes brightened. "Yes, it does. There were three of us. Alfie Dawes, Pete and me. We were great pals, but I only heard this past week that poor old Alfie has passed away. Has Father Pete talked of Alfie?"

"Yes, he has." Said Mother Antonia. "Father Pete prays quite a bit and God forgive me, but he prays far more than could be considered healthy and during those long prayers he often mentions Alfie. He is a very disturbed man."

"Have you any idea why?" Said George.

Mother Antonia bowed her head slightly. "God knows we have tried but it seems that no one can get inside his head. He is fixed on something, or something has fixed on him."

"Are you saying that he is possessed in some way?"

Mother Antonia shuddered. "Heaven forbid but I must admit that I have often thought that to be the case."

"Would it do any good if I spoke with him? Said George.

Mother Antonia sat back in her chair. "Well, it won't do any harm, but I must warn you that if you are not used to being with people like this then it can be quite upsetting. On the other hand, Father Pete may well be having a good day."

Mother Antonia stood up and stepped across the floor.

"If you would like to follow me then." She said as she opened the door.

Her Rosary beads swung lightly from her waist as she swept along the dull, brown and cream corridors. She stopped a few times to speak with patients who seemed to be wandering around, some wearing their dressing gowns, others in their proper day clothes. George stood back, observing as she spoke with them, and she could sense his unease.

"Everyone responds to a smile and a little kindness." She said as she continued leading the way.

A pair of French doors marked the end of their long walk. Sister Antonia swept them open and then she and George were stepping out into a rose garden which was warmed by the sun.

A wiry figure of a man wearing jeans and a beige cardigan was kneeling on the grass, weeding a border with a trowel. Mother Antonia tapped him on the shoulder.

"Father Pete. You have a visitor …. Right, I'll leave you to it." She said with a slight bow of her head.

George stood on the mown grass, looking down at the gaunt, slightly confused face. It's Pete alright, he thought.

"Do you remember me, Pete? …. It's George Murray. Remember us at School, remember the *Alamo*? Pete gave out a small groan as he pushed himself to a stand. The old mischievous grin was still there, even though Pete looked to be years older than his actual age. A Rosary beads and crucifix hung around his neck.

"What have you been doing with yourself, Peter Murphy, in here with all these nuns?"

Pete looked at George for a moment.

"A face from the past ... What are you doing around these parts?" Said Pete, smiling and sounding quite sane.

"What has happened to you Pete? Can I do anything for you? Is it the priesthood? You know you can leave nowadays if you are not happy. It's no big deal anymore, not like the old days when you were stuck with it for life. They can't screw you down like they used to."

Pete shook his head and smiled. "I am happy to serve Christ."

At that moment, the hospital church bell rang. This seemed to have an effect on Pete for his countenance changed and now he looked fearful. He took the Rosary beads from around his neck, knelt on the grass and prayed in a mad sort of frenzy. George watched, perplexed. Poor devil, he thought. He really is in a bad way. He sat on a bench listening to the delirious mumblings as his boyhood friend desperately recited the Rosary.

The prayers had a calming effect on Pete, and he sat beside George.

"That was for you." He said.

"That's very kind of you." Said George.

"You don't understand." Said Pete, whispering.

"Don't understand what?"

Pete took another Rosary from his pocket and pressed the small crucifix into the palm of George's right hand. "You'll need this. Keep it with you always." He said, with a piercing stare.

"You're being very serious, me aul pal." Said George.

Pete gripped George's wrist. "I saw them. I saw evil." Pete grimaced as if physically and mentally trying to back away from some horrifying scene.

"Pete, please tell me what it is you are talking about? What are you afraid of?"

Pete's breathing quickened. His facial muscles seemed to contort as if he was suffering the effects of some weird drug. "Stay away from the *Alamo*! …. Evil …. Pray that Jesus Christ will protect you."

"Protect me from what? Please Pete. You're not making any sense. What is it about Josh Cogan's Farm?"

Pete was praying again now, mumbling, chanting and George knew that he was not going to get any more out of him. Exasperated, he put a hand on Pete's shoulder.

"Take it easy aul pal. I will pray." Said George and he went towards the French doors. But as he did, he turned and looked at the pathetic sight of his boyhood friend mumbling away as if his life depended on it.

Mother Antonia's door was ajar.

"Come in." She said.

George stepped into her office.

"Well, did you get any sense out of him?"

George shook his head. "Not really. He seems to want to warn me about something."

"Have you any idea what that might be?" She said.

"Well, it's a place where we used to play as children. Pete kept telling me to stay away from it."

"The *Alamo?*" Said Mother Antonia. "He talks quite a bit about that place, but he is never specific. He just keeps saying to keep away from the *Alamo*. He just utters the word randomly in his prayers. He also mentions the name Alfie and now come to think of it, he has mentioned the name George too. Could that be yourself?"

It would seem so." Said George. "But how did he end up here in Saint Kevin's?"

"As I said, he'd been in Africa and was sent back here to Ireland to St Vincent's in Ballynamarbh. He was only there a short while when all this happened. Naturally we didn't let it be known to the good people of the parish that their priest had suffered a major mental breakdown, but I do suspect that a few of them know the truth."

George nodded. "Could it be that he had something happen to him in Africa?"

Mother Antonia seemed to bite into her lower lip for a moment and shrugged.

"Mmm …. perhaps. We just don't know. He is a very disturbed man. We can only pray for him."

* * *

It was late afternoon when George arrived back at Ballynamarbh and the Shamrock Hotel. He needed a rest before he would go off to meet the bold Emma Cavendish for the evening, and so he lay on the bed which was still being warmed by the afternoon sun. Although he wanted to sleep for a while, his mind kept going back to Alfie and Pete.

The more he thought about it, the more bizarre it seemed. What was it about his childhood friends that had made their lives go so horribly wrong? Was it just fate or was it something more sinister; something to which he, himself was a party? Sure, he had had his share of bad times and some rotten things had happened to him but nothing that would have made him into a pathetic imbecile or worse, like poor Alfie, made him commit suicide, although he had been close to that himself on at least one occasion in his life. But perhaps his turn hadn't come yet. *Balls*, he thought. If there really was something bad about to happen to him then he would be ready for it.

Refreshed after his rest and a shower, George went down to the bar. The old codger was there on his usual stool, propping up the bar.

"And how's the Dublin man today?" Said the old codger.

"Never better. Been taking the country air." Said George.

They chatted for a while and the old codger had no trouble in getting George to buy the drinks. Then it was time for him to go to meet with Emma Cavendish. He bought a couple of bottles of wine at the bar on his way out.

"Off somewhere special?" Said the old codger.

George smiled but said nothing, leaving the old codger curious.

It was after eight when George left the Shamrock Hotel. He was quite pleased that, for once, he was going to be a bit late. All his life he had been, at the very least, on time for appointments and dates and more often than not, he was ten or even fifteen minutes early. No, he thought, make them wait and they might appreciate him a bit more.

George drove along the short drive that led to the front of Caqueux House. He parked his car beside the yellow Mercedes, took the bottles of wine from the front passenger seat and locked the car. There was no sign of her ladyship, so he headed off through the meadow. The evening sunlight danced on the sea of long yellowy grass and here and there organised swirls of midges seemed to seek him out. The *Alamo* was haunting, its jagged walls spying through the thick green foliage of the trees.

It was quiet, still, whispery as he walked through the woods and into the glade. The sun was at just the right angle to make it look like a scene from a fairy-tale. The cool twinkling light shot a cold shiver through him as if someone had walked on his own grave.

The strong smell of burning wood wafted through the air as he reached the embankment which he climbed, being careful of his footing. The low sunlight seemed to sparkle on the surface of the lake and a fire lit up the place where Emma Cavendish would be. George walked down towards the fire. Orange flames licked into the greying air and sparks flew as the firewood blistered and crackled in the red glow of the flames. George was looking for his hostess. Her figure sat as if meditating, facing out over the lake and towards the almost full moon, now rising in the East.

"Hello." Said George.

Emma Cavendish remained silent. Seeing that she was meditating, George backed off and lit a small cigar. He stood there drawing on the cigar and looking out over the lake. *Bloody women*, he thought, *bloody women; always want to make you wait.* It was several minutes before she finished her meditating. She got to her feet and stood beside George, and they said nothing for a moment as they gazed out over the darkening lake.

"I thought you might sit with me." She said.

"I'm afraid I'm not very much into that sort of thing. What is it, meditation?"

"Yes, it heals the spirit. It puts you in touch with the universe, transcends time….. not just the here and now. The dimensions of your mind become boundless.

"I'll take your word about that." He smiled. "I have brought some wine. Would you like a glass? I am presuming that you have a corkscrew and glasses here."

"Actually, I have a bottle on the go. So here, have a glass of mine."

She pulled a bottle from a cool box and poured two glasses.

"You think of everything. Don't you." Said George.

She smiled. "You want to try the hammock?"

George sat into the hammock, being conscious that he could make a fool of himself and fall right out, landing face down in the dirt but he managed to do it without much fuss. Emma handed a glass of wine to him, and she sat on a log next to the hammock.

"You hungry?" She said.

"Kind of." Said George as he watched the faint twinkling of stars in the darkening sky.

"I have trout, from this very lake." Said Emma.

A tranquillity settled over George as he swayed gently from side to side. Emma served up the fish which had been baking in foil in the hot cinders. Another foil contained baked vegetables. They ate like cowboys out on the range.

"You know." Said George. "I always wanted to eat like this. I tried it once as a boy with beans. I wanted to be a cowboy."

"You had a good boyhood?" Said Emma, the flames from the fire reflecting in her eyes.

"I certainly did. Hated girls though." He said with a smile.

"And now?" She said.

He smiled again. "Can you pick out the North Star?"

Emma looked up. "Oh yes." She raised her slender arm towards the sky, drawing directions from star to star. "See it there?"

The burning wood collapsed into a heap of sparking red-hot cinders, disturbing their astronomical studies. Emma filled the wine glasses again and they sipped contentedly, happy to just gaze at the glowing ashes while the Moon spied through some lose clouds above the eastern horizon. Emma jumped to her feet. "Come on. Let's go for a row on the lake." She said excitedly as she skipped towards the little rowing boat.

"Jesus! The water is freezing." Said George, plodding barefoot through the stony shallows as he pushed the little boat to deeper water. He jumped in at the stern giving the little boat some momentum as he did. Emma had already taken the oars and was quickly in full rhythm with easy efficient strokes.

"You do that very well." Said George.

"Practice!"

A woeful wooing sound came from somewhere across the lake.

"Sounds as if some poor creature is in pain." Said George.

"Or having fun." Said Emma, her darkened figure firmly in tune with the oars and the waters of the lake.

The clouds had retreated to the edges of the sky, giving the moon its own clear patch of territory. There was no breeze now and the surface of the lake was like ink; black and shiny. Emma stopped rowing. A meteor streaked across a corner of the sky, fizzling out in an instant.

"Did you see that?" Said Emma. "Beautiful."

"Will there be more?" Said George.

"If you are very good."

"An expert on the sky and nature. What else are you good at?" He said.

She grinned smugly and then they were silent for a while. Drops of water fell from the blades of the resting oars and the moon reflected perfectly in each drop, sending tiny ripples of dissolving moonlight into the glossy, inky water. George felt Emma's stare which briefly made him feel self-conscious. In the blink of an eye, another meteor darted along, its trail of speckled bright fire fizzling out as quickly as it appeared.

"Another one." Said George. "Did you see it?"

The little boat drifted gently as the crew gazed into the star speckled heavens with the darkened horizon all around them.

"Your turn." Said Emma, as she left her seat at the centre of the boat and sat at the stern. The little boat rocked a bit and then it rocked again as George moved forward to take up the oars.

"It's years since I did this." He said, grappling to get a proper rhythm.

"Oh, it's just like riding a bike. You never forget." Said Emma. Her voice was more of a whisper now, enchanting as if she and the lake and the sky were as one.

It was only a few hundred yards or so back to the shore but after a short while George's arms began to ache. He was glad when the little boat finally bumped to a stop on the stones near the dying fire.

"Looks like someone had a party." She joked. "I wonder who?"

Emma scooped a bucket of water from the lake and threw it on the fire, sending squealing clouds of steam into the night air. George sat on a large stone, struggling awkwardly as he pulled his socks over his feet.

"Come on." Said Emma and she ran towards the old railway embankment. She was almost at the top before George could finish tying his shoelaces. He chased after her as her dark figure went down the other side and disappeared into the night. George walked on, hurrying as he followed the way back towards Caqueux, but he wasn't going to run, not in the darkness. Then he was at the edge of the glade.

The moon, shining through the tops of the trees, made a haunting silver shadowy oil painting of the glade. The moonlight allowed him to see Emma who was sitting in the middle of the glade, her knees tucked up beneath her chin and her arms wrapped around her folded legs. George walked slowly towards her and eased himself down to sit near to her. Their figures cast clear shadows which emphasised the contrast between his masculine hulk and her feminine gracefulness. George began to say something, but she immediately silenced him by putting her fingers over his lips.

Emma stood up and keeping her eyes on his face, she pressed her right foot against his shoulder, gently forcing him to lie on his back. Her towering outline silhouetted against the moonlight as she stood straddled over him. He was about to say something but again she quelled him, this time with her bare foot over his mouth. George kissed and caressed the petite slender foot. Then both his hands were around her ankles, slowly sliding along the firm, smooth flesh on her legs. Emma flung her head back, wallowing in the adoration.

Her light summer dress loosened as if she had willed it to do so and then the dress fell onto the eager man beneath her. She was completely naked. She didn't let him move from the spot. He looked up the length of her body as she moved in spellbinding gyrations until she felt adored enough. Then she joined him on the grass, slowly and teasingly undressing him as if it were an art. They made love beneath the ghostly moonlight on a heavenly carpet of green grass near to the mound of earth that looked like a grave.

* * *

A cold chill and the sound of chirping birds woke George. His clothes were strewn about the glade. Emma wasn't there. He called her name aloud; nothing but the sound of the birds. He shivered, piecing the night together in his mind, wondering how long he had been there.

The grey light vanished as the morning sunlight covered the countryside with colour and warmth. Where had Emma gone? George wondered. Had he been out there all night and not felt the cold until now? He was puzzled but smiled to himself as he remembered the intense pleasures of sometime in the past few hours. Was it minutes or hours before? He didn't really know. Was it all a very nice dream? He caught a whiff of her perfume as it lingered on his body. It was almost as if she had left a deliberate reminder of the pleasure which she had bestowed on him.

George looked at the mound where a Gipsy was supposed to have been buried. For some reason he felt that he was trespassing. He stumbled about, pulling on his trousers with the elated feeling of having made the best love, ever. Was it all a dream? Why had she left? Ah! Women, he thought. He would never understand them.

He went back through the woods and climbed the old railway embankment from where he could see the trees by the lakeside with the hammock and the little punt. Definitely not a dream, he muttered. Dishevelled, he continued along the old rail line, back towards Ballynamarbh.

A little while later he was walking along the road that took him under the bridge to the village. Not a sound. The Main Street was shrouded in its early morning silence, waiting for people to bring it to life. Daydreaming, George passed the Shamrock Hotel without really noticing it. Then he was at the entrance to the churchyard. It was as if he were being drawn there. The headstones jutted through the wispy morning mist. Then he was gazing into the newer graveyard and towards where Alfie was buried. He focused on the grave and a voice came into his head. "*Beware the blue moon.*" He slapped his hands over his ears in an attempt to end this bad dream, but this wasn't some bad dream. This was all too real.

The low-lying mist cleared, showing a path between the headstones. George peered in disbelief and for a moment he was caught in a trance as a small boy stood staring at him. He wasn't able to see the boy's features clearly except that he was shaking his head as if saying *no*. The mist closed in as quickly as it had cleared, and the boy was not there. George ran along the path, stopping where he thought the boy had been standing. But there was no one there. He called out.

There was nothing there; nothing except his own voice, intrusive among the sacred, silent headstones and the thinning mist. He ran further among the headstones. He was at the end of the path now with only a field before him, disappearing into the still slumbering countryside. He was very confused.

George went back to Alfie's grave. He blessed himself and said a prayer as if asking his dead childhood friend for help. The grave and the headstone remained silent, but the voice came into his head again. *"Beware the blue moon."*

He shook his head and then he remembered the Tinker girl from all those years before with her haunting pointing finger. A distant echoing bark from some distant dog disturbed his thoughts, as if calling him back to the present.

* * *

The night porter seemed to be hovering around the reception desk at the hotel. George nodded acknowledgment; conscious of his tired, unshaven face and ruffled hair. He grabbed the banisters of the wide staircase with his left hand, almost pulling himself upwards with a hurried but exhausted motion.

The hotel room was a warm peaceful haven after the ecstasy and bewilderment of the previous few hours. He avoided looking at himself in the mirror. Mirrors have a haunting quality of their own. Other worlds exist in mirrors, infinities, parallel universes, demons of the mind and if he did dare to gaze at his own reflection then he might see something other than his own reflection, something that might scare the hell out of him, and he had had enough frightening apparitions for one day. He threw off his clothes, letting them fall in a heap and he slid between the sheets and the cossetting embrace of the duvet. He laid there, his exhausted body wanting to sleep but his mind was agitated, racing, bothered by what he had seen or thought he had seen. He just wasn't sure. The Rosary beads with the crucifix, which Pete had given him, had fallen from his trouser pocket and as it lay on the floor, George's eyes focussed on the crucifix.

The mournful, laborious gongs of the church bells for the midday Angelus woke George from his half-sleep as his mind anticipated each strike of the bell with each singular gong receding into its own silent death. He wanted to stay in bed where he felt warm and safe. *Better get up*, he thought, as this cocooning wasn't making his thoughts any less upsetting. He stepped into the shower, lingering there for several minutes with the warm water beating off his face and shoulders. He dried himself and then he blessed himself before confronting the mirror.

Bloodshot eyes stared back at him. An old man! He thought. His hands were trembling as he began to shave. A stinging sensation shot through the skin below his chin where the razor blade had just been. It seemed ok for a brief second, but the inevitable red line of blood appeared as the surface of the skin split apart. *Clumsy! Need that check-up*, he thought, determining that he would have one that very day.

Three messages were waiting for George at the hotel reception desk. One was from his business partner, Larry, asking him to phone back. One was from Emma Cavendish, telling him that he had left his car at Caqueux House and inviting him to … *a small party on the following* evening …. and the third message was from Lisa, asking if he could contact her. George didn't really want to talk to anyone, especially Lisa. What he really needed was someone, anyone with an understanding of the paranormal or whatever the hell he had seen or thought he had seen.

George sat in a corner of the bar at the Shamrock Hotel, thinking back over the events of the past few days. There was the strange, alluring Emma Cavendish, the ghostly sightings, the graveyard. There was the blood on the wall at the *Alamo,* whispers in the night air, a childhood friend who was dead and another in an asylum. What did it all add up to? Was he going insane, himself? Then there was the photograph. *Weird, all so bloody weird.* There must be some logical explanation, he thought and now Miss Lisa was trying to contact him …. *Well, she can go to hell.*

Emma's voice seemed to soothe away his cares as they spoke over the phone. George mentioned the valuation and the report that he was yet to do but she didn't seem that bothered about the property, and she hoped that she would see him the following evening, this time at Caqueux House and that she would be having other guests in. "And by the way," she said, "great night, last night." Then she hung up, having had the last word.

Doctor Mitchell's surgery was located in a cul-de-sac near to the school. Two old women and an old man looked at George as he came into the waiting room. They stared at the stranger for a moment or two, then continued reading their magazines. The pile of magazines on the low table reminded George of the barber's shop where he used to go as a boy. He cringed as he thought of the *boring* old Punch magazines. As a child, he could never understand how anyone in their right mind would ever read anything without pictures and *surely the horrible Punch magazines were put into barbers' shops, especially to torment small, fun-loving boys*. Even now, as an adult, the thought of his boyhood visits to the barber's sent a shiver up the back of his neck. He could still feel those torturous cold clippers as the insensitive, white-coated man *lawn-mowered* the back of his head, leaving the cold air to rush against his raw blue skin. He remembered how the barber would almost drown him by covering whatever was left of his hair with cold sticky hair oil. He would come out of the barber's shop into the freezing cold, feeling as if his head had been peeled like an orange.

The second hand on the clock of the doctor's waiting room went round and round as the minutes dragged themselves forward. George studied the faces of the elderly people who were waiting patiently for their turn. The old man looked as if he had spent his whole life in pain with his stubbly, furrowed face beneath a well fingered, greasy cloth cap. He wheezed every so often as if the whole world should know about his suffering. The women sat bulging through their summer coats. One of them wore a grey tammy hat which was filled-out by her hair. The other woman looked as if a visit to the doctor was just another part of her social life.

One by one, they were called and one by one, they creaked off into the surgery where they recited their aches and pains to the weary doctor. Then it was George's turn. Doctor Mitchell looked as old as the previous patients.

"So, what seems to be the trouble?" Said Doctor Mitchell.

George was a bit reluctant to come clean. *He'll probably think I'm mad.* George thought.

"Oh, I've just been feeling a little off colour." Said George. "Thought it best to come for a check-up."

"I see." Said the doctor as he prodded around George's throat.

He asked George to open his shirt. The stethoscope was cool against his skin.

"Do you smoke?"

"Only the odd cigar." Said George, trying to make it sound insignificant.

"And drink?"

George nodded. "Yes, probably a bit too much of late."

"I see."

"Well, I did lose my girlfriend recently."

"Ah!" Said the doctor as if he had pinpointed the problem. "Take a deep breath."

The doctor finished his examination and George buttoned up his shirt. After a brief chat about George's broken romance, the examination was over. George did feel better now that it was confirmed that he wasn't about to drop dead, but it was more the cathartic nature of his unburdening that helped most.

* * *

Back at the hotel, George ordered tea and toast. Hot, sweet tea always does the trick, he said to himself as he sat in the garden with the warm sun on his back and the calming chirping of small birds as they grubbed among the shrubs.

But it wasn't long before his thoughts drifted back to the weird happenings and so in an attempt to take his mind off this, he went to his room to write his report on Caqueux House. Curious about the name, he consulted his dictionary. Caqueux … Caqueux … Caqueux. He thumbed down the columns. And there it was. Caqueux; a Gipsy tribe from Brittany. Interesting, he thought

The Tinker girl came into his head again. *Could it be ….? Naw, coincidence, sheer coincidence.* He began to describe the location as part of his report and then he described the house itself. He found himself knowing each sentence before he actually thought it, or it was as if someone or something was actually guiding the pen in his hand. His hand moved over the paper and what came from the nib of the pen astounded

him. He read it back to himself, not believing his own eyes
..... *Beware the Blue Moon* ..... scrawled across the page.
George dropped the pen, cradling his face in both hands.
Childlike; he rubbed his eyes to look at the page again, but
the warning had gone, disappeared as if it had never been
there at all.

He felt exhausted again, as if he had been drained of his
energy. George let the papers fall to the floor and he lay back
and fell asleep on the bed.

It was later that night when he woke. He pointed the
remote control at the television set. Fuzziness flickered
annoyingly on the screen. He went through the channels
but nothing. George showered and got dressed.

"Off again?" Said the old codger, who was propping up
the bar, as George passed through on his way out of the hotel.
George gave a wave and kept going. The old codger looked
disappointed. He wasn't going to have any free drink that
night.

George set off, on foot towards, Caqueux House where
he had left his car. His jacket felt quite damp by the time
he reached the house. He had walked through a mist for a
good part of the way, but he didn't realise that it had been
so dense. His car was where he had left it the night before,
at the front of the house but there was no sign of the yellow
Mercedes or of the blue Land Rover. The house itself was in
darkness; its glassy, inky windows keeping watch and spying
into the night. He was tempted to see if anyone was at home,

but he thought better of it. He sat into the car and drove away.

* * *

The national anthem played, ending television programmes from Radio Telefís Éireann for the night. Garda Phil Keane's television buzzed noisily as he dozed lightly on the couch. He opened his eyes, his pale sleep ridden face staring into space. He was alone again, an empty glass next to a half empty bottle of Irish whiskey on the coffee table beside him. Now, it wasn't that he had taken to the bottle completely, but of late he had been drinking a bit more than was good for him. He didn't want to go to bed, to go upstairs to that lonely bedroom which he had shared with his beloved wife Mary for nearly three decades.

Phil Keane looked across to the sideboard with its array of framed photographs. Himself and Mary on their wedding day, the boys when they were just babies and again as grown men and one of Mary on her own, smiling out at him; his favourite photograph of her.

Mary had gone now; dead this past two years and he wasn't any nearer to getting used to it. One of the boys had gone off to California and the other had settled in Sydney. Phil wondered, as he had so often wondered of late, as to what it was it all about? Having had such a settled life with a good career and a wonderful family, now he was alone and lonely with only his memories to comfort or torment him.

One year to go, he told himself, just one more year as a Garda Sergeant at Ballynamarbh. Then what would he do? End his days like the old guys who propped up the bar over at the Shamrock Hotel. Policing this small rural community was all he knew, his only interest. Even when he was off duty and was supposed to be relaxing, he still wore his light blue Garda shirt and navy trousers. He pushed himself up off the couch with a groan. He looked at the mirror, straightening his tie and he slipped into his tunic. Might as well get some air, he thought.

It was mild outside, a covering of cloud keeping the day's heat from dispersing into the atmosphere. Garda Phil Keane walked along the narrow lane that led from his house to Ballynamarbh's main street. A couple of tomcats glared at each other in a territorial standoff. Phil stood beneath the streetlight outside the Garda station, looking along the quiet street. Ballynamarbh still wasn't a bad place to be, he thought, still peaceful at night, passed over by the modern world in many respects. He had thought of leaving when Mary died, of going off to Australia with his son and young family. But no, when it came down to it, he just couldn't bear to leave the village where he had spent the greater part of his life with the woman he adored. Even though it was very painful at times, he preferred to be near all those places where they shared so much of their lives. No, he would die here and be buried in the earth at St Vincent's church, next to his wife and if the rest of his days were to be an unhappy empty existence, then so be it; his reward of eternity with Mary, would surely come.

The lights of a car came from beneath the old railway bridge. The indicator flashed and the driver pulled up, parking just beyond where Phil was standing. George Murray stepped out of the car and nodded to Phil.

"Good night." Said George as he crossed the street towards the hotel. Phil nodded. "Good night," and he turned to face the Garda station.

The Garda station was in darkness. Phil could have sworn that he saw someone at one of the windows. He took the bunch keys from his belt, held them towards the streetlight and selected the one for the main entrance.

He pushed at the heavy outer door, and he stepped inside, closing it behind him. He switched the light on in the lobby, thinking that he had heard a noise, but he couldn't be sure as the old building was a bit creaky anyway. He went into the front office. There was no one there, only the two desks with their black phones and curled-up wires, stacks of files and that stale papery, pencil smell like some old chalky school room.

He stepped back into the lobby with is blistering cream walls which led up the dusty wooden stairway to the darkened first floor landing. It was silent, eerie, his footsteps disturbing the air as he moved past the stairs towards the small cell at the rear of the station where he would occasionally have to put a drunk driver or some such offender, for the night.

He slid his hand over the peeling paintwork next to the cell until it found the light switch. The light in the cell came on. He looked through the bars of the unlocked cell and suddenly he froze, petrified.

Phil Keane had no words for what he was now seeing. He gasped in horror at the young man sitting on the cell bunk. The man was laughing at him, a cynical mad laugh. But the laughing wasn't the problem. The problem was that the young man had died some fifteen years before. Phil blessed himself and quickly moved backwards towards the lobby. In a panic, he turned and ran.

Phil Keane was outside again now, safe in the open, even though it was the dead of night. He could hear his own heart as it pounded away inside his chest. He knew that he had seen a ghost, the ghost of Jamey Cronin. His mind turned back to the time some fifteen years before when he first encountered Jamey Cronin. He remembered so very well, and why wouldn't he. After all he was the man who arrested him.

A child from the village had been murdered. The entire community was in uproar and looking for blood and as is generally the way with mob hysteria, just about anyone's blood would do. Phil remembered that night so well now, not that he could ever forget. Phil and a colleague went down to a Traveller family that had camped near the village that winter. Jamey Cronin was the only young able bodied, adult male member of that Tinker family. Jamey Cronin; the most obvious suspect …. *Of course, he did it …. bloody Tinkers ….*

animals …. string him up …. castrate him …. drown the whole feckin lot of 'em …. was the overwhelming consensus of the good Christian people of Ballynamarbh.

The howling, shouting, abusive mob had gathered at the Garda station as Phil Keane brought the man in for questioning. Jamey was only eighteen or twenty at the most and he was and looked scared to death. He shivered and shook nervously during the Garda interview. Phil Keane remembered it so well; how Jamey denied in his own pathetic, inarticulate way that he had anything to do with the terrible crime. The interview was inconclusive. Further investigations were needed and besides, detectives from Dublin were on their way to take up the case but in the meantime, he thought it best to keep Jamey Cronin in a locked cell, not least for his own protection.

It was less than an hour later when Phil found Jamey Cronin dead in the cell. He was hanging from a rope made of torn bedding which Jamey had tied to the bars on the window, six feet above the floor. The angry villagers' tribal hunger for vengeance was satiated. A few days later the real culprit was arrested. But that was no help to the wretched Jamey Cronin, no help or consolation at all. He was dead, his young life had gone forever, and Phil Keane was left to live with his conscience. Could he not have stayed with Jamey or watched him while he was in the cell? He should have made sure that the lad was ok. But he didn't and ever since, Phil Keane had to live with the decisions he made that fateful night.

Phil poured yet another whiskey for himself and sat upright on the couch. He was still in a daze, trying to make sense of what he had seen or thought he had seen. He had never believed in ghosts. Perhaps it was his memory playing tricks. Perhaps it was the light. He couldn't really say, but whatever it was, he wasn't going to discuss it with anyone … *the local cop losing it… going nuts.* He could hear them saying it. No, this was something he would have to keep to himself.

* * *

George needed some answers. His physical health seemed to be ok, and he didn't think he was going out of his mind. He expected weird escapades when he had had a few too many drinks or when he was hungover but when he was sober, stone cold sober …. he was sober. *No*, he told himself, *he was definitely not falling off his perch.*

He was wide awake. It was four o'clock in the morning; his mind was racing, his thoughts jumping about from Lisa to ghosts to the very seductive Emma Cavendish and back again to Lisa. He tried to get some sleep and maybe he did, but it felt as if he didn't.

He went down for breakfast at about nine o'clock. There were different people in the breakfast room that morning. The tourists, the Yanks, the Germans and the other couple had all left Ballynamrabh, gone off to explore other parts of the country.

There must be some rational explanation for all these strange happenings, he thought as he breakfasted on bacon and eggs. Should he go back to the doctor? No; maybe the priest? Yes, he reckoned, the priest, just up the road. He should know something. After all, this was his parish, his village and his business and if there really were supernatural happenings in the district then the priest should surely know.

Breakfast eaten, George walked up to St Vincent's and knocked on the presbytery door. The priest, he had met a few days earlier, opened the door and stood there looking at George for moment.

"Hello …. Father Casey, isn't it?"

"Yes, what can I do for you?" He said, looking at his watch as if no one ever called at this early hour in the day.

"Can we have a word, Father? I think you might be able to help me."

"Look, I'm a bit busy today …."

"Father, just a few minutes, please."

"I'm sorry." Said the priest as he tried to close the door.

George quickly jammed his foot between the door and the frame.

"Father. It is important. Now, I need to talk, and I have a feeling that you might be able to answer some of my questions."

Father Casey thought for a moment. "Alright, you had better come in."

Shelves of books lined the walls in Father Casey's untidy Victorian study which smelt of stale tobacco smoke. He motioned George to sit in one of the armchairs.

"You should leave Ballynamarbh." Said the priest.

"And why's that?" Said George. "What exactly do you know that I don't?"

Father Casey moved some books on a coffee-table as he searched for his packet of cigarettes. He offered one to George who declined and then took one for himself, tapped the end against the packet and put it between his lips. The cigarette-end glowed red as he addictively drew on it, sucking back a lungful of smoke before exhaling. "You've been to see Mother Antonia." He said.

"Yes, I have." Said George. "But I was given to understand that my visit there was confidential."

"And it was …. is. But Mother Antonia keeps me informed about Father Murphy's condition…. I, being his successor here in Ballynamarbh."

Relaxed somewhat, Father Casey seemed to be a bit more cooperative now.

"So, tell me, exactly what is going on here, Father? Since I arrived here a few days ago, I have been having these weird experiences. Do you believe in ghosts, or could it be that for some reason, I am losing my mind?"

Father Casey paused for a moment. "The straight answer to that is yes. Yes, you could well have seen a ghost or ghosts in this village." He stared across the room through the window for a moment. "It's not so much ghosts. In most cases ghosts are fairly harmless." He paused again.

"But?" Said George.

Father Casey shook his head. "Before I go any further, I need your word that you will keep this conversation to yourself. The last thing we need is a panic in this village or worse; hordes of journalists and ghoulish sightseers wandering around."

George nodded. "Of course."

"Well, it's evil that is the big danger here." Said Father Casey.

A confused look came over George. "What do you mean, evil?"

"Exactly what I say, a force of Satan. We believe that, for some reason, it has chosen to impose itself on us here in this village and the surrounding townlands."

George smiled cynically. "You're having me on?"

The priest shook his head. "Well, you did ask me, and I am answering as truthfully as I can."

"I'm sorry." Said George. "I didn't mean to …."

"And you for some reason, along with Father Peter Murphy and Alfie Dawes, God rest him, were chosen or are connected in some way with what is going on."

"How do you know all this?" Said George.

Father Casey sucked the last drag from his cigarette before stubbing the butt in his ashtray. "There is a background to all this, if you have time to listen?"

"All day if you want." Said George.

"Well, we have done quite a bit of research on this."

"Wait a minute." Said George. "Who's we?"

"Myself and Father Thwaites."

"Father Thwaites?" Said George, as the penny was about to drop.

"Yes." Said Father Casey. "Father Arthur Thwaites. He is in Caqueux at the moment. Undercover, you might say."

"So, Thwaites is one of yours?"

"He is." Said Father Casey. "Anyway, as I was saying, I'll tell you what we know. We are talking history here, hundreds of years. Let me take you back to the time of the French revolution, the end of the eighteenth century … It seems that a Gipsy family were on the run from the revolutionaries. It's not known why but we think the revolutionaries may have thought that our Gipsy family were actually aristocrats in disguise. But they were really Gipsies from Brittany, Caqueux as they were known. However, the noose was tightening. You must remember that much of France at the time was probably something like Nazi occupied Europe with curfews, martial law, fear etc. Anyway, the entire family; men, women, children were being hunted down, so they were in fear of their lives. It seems they made it to the coast and were able to steal a boat of some sort. The story goes that they put to sea in the middle of the night and sailed or drifted for perhaps weeks, finally landing on the south coast of Ireland."

Father Casey left his chair and opened a cabinet, taking a bottle of Irish whiskey from the shelf. He poured two quarter tumblers of the whiskey and handed one to George. He sat down again. "It's early in the day but I think we both need this."

They both took a mouthful.

"So, they made it to Ireland?" Said George.

Father Casey balanced his glass on the arm of his chair, circling the tip of his right middle finger around the rim.

"Oh, they reached Ireland alright. But the only reference we have to a date is the Full Moon. Now, whether it was a fact or not, subsequent folklore has made that into a Blue Moon. Do you know what a blue moon is?"

George shook his head. "No. Tell me."

"It's when there are two Full Moons in the same calendar month. The second one is known as the Blue Moon."

"I see." Said George, sipping his whiskey.

"Well, stories have it that these French Gipsies landed on the coast a few miles along from Polglas. They are supposed to have come in with the tide. They must have been so relieved to have reached land, but they didn't know where they were. They were spotted by the locals and followed."

"What sort of reception did they get?" Said George.

"Well, it wasn't a very Christian welcome."

"So, what happened?"

The Gipsies headed inland for a few miles and found a farmhouse where they asked for food. They were starving, thirsty and weak. Then the locals confronted them. Well, you can imagine …. what was it, the end of the seventeen-hundreds? Few people ever came across foreigners. Even people from fifty miles away were foreign in those days. Just imagine, you're an Irish peasant, working the land, minding your own business. You've never been more than about five, ten miles from the place where you were born and reared. Suddenly you see a gang of well-tanned, dark haired creatures all wearing rags, speaking some odd language, looking hungry as wolves, all making their way towards your measly little straw corner of this world. What would you think? What would you do?"

George smiled his understanding.

"Exactly." Said Father Casey. "You'd panic at the very least, wouldn't you? Our local peasants let their tribal instincts rule. A gang of them chased the wretched refugees. At that time there were only a few stone cottages and a small church here in Ballynamarbh. Anyway, the Gipsy family ran to the church hoping for asylum. The pastor or whoever was in charge, refused to give them asylum and so the local peasants chased these poor unfortunates out of the church and into the fields to a place, near where Caqueux House now stands, where they clubbed them all to death, men, women, children. That is the story as far as we know and a very ugly story it is too.

The ticking of the clock on the mantelpiece disturbed the momentary pensive silence between them.

"You know what Ballynamarbh means?" Said father Casey.

"You know, I never thought about it." Said George.

"Do you know your Irish? Baile na Marbh. It means the town of the dead."

"Was that because of the massacre?" Said George. "But what has all that got to do with now; evil and all that, ghosts and things? I don't understand."

Father Casey took another cigarette, repeating the ritual of tapping the tip against the packet before putting it between his lips and lighting it. "We don't quite understand ourselves. We think we are dealing with the forces of evil. Because of the massacre, the sheer brutality of it and the betrayal by our fellow Christians and a priest at that, we think that evil has had a reason to come to this place. We think this evil is using the unsettled souls of the Gipsies to manifest itself."

"How do you know?" Said George.

Father Casey took a moment …. thinking. "Well, I'm guessing that Mother Antonia didn't tell you everything. Apart from the folklore, which is common knowledge in the area, along with our own research, we do know quite a bit about what happened to Peter Murphy. Father Thwaites spent some time with him in St Kevin's. It seems that when Peter came back from Africa and began his work here, he went walking in the meadow at Caqueux House. It was there that whatever happened to him, happened."

George sat up in his seat. "So, what did happen to him?"

"He saw something from the past. We believe he saw the scene from when the Gipsies were hounded from the sanctuary of the church. In one of Peter's more lucid moments, he told Father Thwaites of seeing a foreign looking girl being chased across the fields. The young girl was pregnant, her belly quite swollen. Father Pete described the scene vividly. A gang of the locals chased her. When they caught her, they hacked the poor little thing to pieces, spilling the innocent unborn onto the earth. Father Pete described the scene with a fear that made it seem as if he had been there himself and even that he could have actually taken part in the gruesome lynching. He claims that he saw some grotesque creature in the midst of all that violence. We think that that creature was some satanic apparition. But whatever it was, it has affected the poor man so much that his mind cannot deal with it, rendering him an idiot for most of the time."

"Did any of the Gipsies escape?" Said George.

Father Casey let out a deep sigh. "We don't really know for sure. It is said that one of the male children survived and was taken in by a cattleman and his wife who lived in a cottage where Caqueux House now stands. It is said that the cattleman and his wife, having no children of their own, kept the little Gipsy boy who grew up and eventually inherited the rights to the small holding. But no one knows or has ever admitted to knowing where the bodies of those who were murdered are buried. That has always been the big mystery."

"So, tell me, how does all this affect events of today?" Said George.

"They say that the French boy married and through his descendants, there has always been a direct line from the Gipsy family right down to the last owner of Caqueux House."

"Josh Cogan, right?" Said George.

"That's right and this is where Arthur Thwaites comes in. He has spent his life, since becoming a priest, learning about the paranormal and the forces of evil. As I myself have, incidentally." Father Casey shrugged. "Anyway, Arthur came over from England to meet Father Pete. The moment he arrived in Caqueux, he says he could almost smell the evil as if it was taunting him to have a go. That sense or feeling was all around, in the house and in the meadow and in the old derelict farm building near the meadow. He knew that something was very wrong. With him, it is as if he represents the Christ, as if he has been singled out for the job."

"And where does Emma Cavendish fit in?" Said George.

Father Casey left his chair and went to the end of the room, he turned to George. His countenance was serious again.

"Josh Cogan had no heir. The line from the French Gipsy boy ended with him. Now, what I've told you so far could be just a story, a tale, or a myth." He shrugged. "You can believe it or not. But when it comes to Emma Cavendish well, that's where the whole thing becomes really sinister. Now so far, I have told you these things because you insisted."

George nodded. "That is correct."

"Not only that but you will recall that Father Thwaites did not seem very enthusiastic about having you visit Caqueux House."

"That's right." Said George.

"Initially, we didn't want you around here but since you have come this far, and you have shown a deep interest then you might be able to help us. You see, Arthur is of the opinion that this Emma Cavendish is his opposite. She was, he is sure, sent in by the opposite forces."

"I don't understand." Said George.

"Well, if Arthur is, shall we say the eyes and the ears of Christ, then she is his exact opposite; the agent of the Antichrist."

George stared into Father Casey's eyes for a long moment.

"Are you telling me that we are dealing with some kind of she-devil?"

"Most certainly." Said father Casey.

"I really can't believe that." Said George, shaking his head.

"No, …. then tell me why you came back here after a lifetime, what …. thirty odd years?"

George thought for a moment. He shrugged. "Well, I first came across her at an auction which I was conducting at my offices in Dublin. She bought a picture, a painting of the Full Moon…." He stopped in mid-sentence as if the penny were dropping …. "You don't think she made all this happen? Do you?"

"I do, and what's more that painting is part of her armoury." Said father Casey.

"What do you mean?"

"I mean the painting depicts the meadow at Caqueux. It seems that the artist managed to capture not only what he saw in his present time, but simultaneously, the very same meadow at another moment in a former time."

Father Casey moved to the other end of the room and pulled open a drawer from which he took a bottle of holy water along with a Rosary. Like some wise old sage imparting a vital wisdom, he gave them to George.

"You'll need these if you are going back there. I take it you are going back there?"

A confused look came over George. "Yes, she has invited me there tonight." He looked at his watch. "It all sounded so innocent."

"I suppose it did. Just remember that she is a very dangerous person, or creature."

"What do you think will happen there?" Said George.

"There will be a Full Moon tonight, the second of the month, a Blue Moon. Our guess is that she will want to perform some kind of ritual."

"Black magic or something?" Said George.

"Yes." Said father Casey with a fearful look on his face,

"But why me? What's so special about me?"

"That's what we hope to find out. Father Thwaites will be there, observing from a distance."

"Do I have to go there?" Said George.

Father Casey didn't answer that. He just looked at George and George himself had a feeling that he had to go anyway, as if it had already been ordained that he should. They left the presbytery, stepped out into the sunshine and walked across to the church.

* * *

Arthur Thwaites pulled back the rug which lay beside his bed. A small length of the floorboards was kept in place with two screws. Arthur removed the screws. Here, beneath the dusty floorboards, Arthur Thwaites kept hidden his sacred vestments, a small bottle of altar wine, a chalice, communion wafers, a candle and holy oils.

He pulled on the vestments and laid a white cloth on a worktop. He placed the chalice, the wine and the wafers on the cloth. Nervously, he checked again to see that the door was locked and that the curtains were drawn fully. He stood before the makeshift altar, kissed the stole which he put around his neck, then he began to say Mass.

Arthur had lived like this since he arrived at Caqueux; posing as a right-hand man for Emma Cavendish while secretly offering the sacrifice of the Mass. He often wondered if she knew who he really was. After all, she did have supernatural powers and perhaps she was merely playing with him. Arthur had to dig deep into his spiritual reserves to combat the evil that he felt around him each day. Sometimes he wondered if there really was a difference between good and evil; just another war, a throwback from the creation or whatever unevenness was necessary to kick start the long endless adventure of human evolution. He had to fight such thoughts for he knew that his mind was being infiltrated. *Shut them out, shut them out. Say a prayer ... stay with me Jesus, dear Jesus, stay with me ...* He would mumble to himself. His faith would bring him through, he knew it would, he knew that Jesus Christ was looking over him.

When he had finished saying Mass, he put all his holy vestments and instruments back into their hiding place beneath the floorboards, then replaced the screws and the rug. He knelt beside his bed and prayed intently for a long while.

* * *

The grass was wet as Arthur took Sammy for a walk across the meadow. The old dog jostled and pranced about, chasing a well chewed tennis ball which his master hurled into the distance for him. Spying all this; Emma Cavendish stood at her bedroom window, her eyes fixed as she watched Arthur and the dog as they approached the *Alamo*. Arthur followed Sammy as he ran onto the old ruins. He called out; *Sammy, here boy, Sammy, Sammy, where have you gone?*

A terrible feeling of doom came over Arthur and he immediately crossed himself. Suddenly he was unable move as if he had become fixed to the spot on the dirt floor between the jagged crumbling walls of the old farm building. Then the walls were swirling about him as if he were at the centre of some hideous carousel. In his desperation, he tried to recite the Hail Mary, but the words just would not come. His mind was thinking the words, but his lips and his tongue refused to utter them. Deeply afraid now, he switched his mind to think …. *Christ, stay with me, Christ stay with me, Christ stay with me.* He tried to take his Rosary beads from his pocket, but his arms wouldn't move, and his hands seemed as if they had stiffened in concrete gloves. He felt he was doomed. He felt he was close to death as the old walls spun around him, as if they too were in some horrific agony. Arthur heard screams; men, women and children; all crying out, all in fear of their lives.

The noise stopped and the *Alamo* was still again. Arthur was exhausted. His heart was pounding, his breathing was an agony of short painful gasps. He needed time to be able to recover from whatever had just happened to him. He could move his limbs again. He leaned his upper body forward, rubbing his face as he mentally thanked God that he was still ok, still alive.

"Sammy! ….. Where have you been? Boy, did I need you?"

Sammy just stood there, defiant with a mesmerising, beastly stare. A groaning came from deep within the hound. The groaning grew into a howl, the howl of a mad beast. Arthur knew that this was it. He would have no chance against this dog whose eyes were now blood red with an evil rage.

"No, Sammy. No." Arthur shouted in his desperation. With a powerful leap, the mad dog brought his master to the ground. Arthur's last vision was of Emma Cavendish as she stood in the opening, watching the savage attack.

"Good boy, Sammy." She said, standing over Arthur's body as it lay dead on the dirt floor. His throat had been ripped open, leaving a mess of torn twisted flesh with rivulets of blood trickling into the dirt.

Sammy whimpered about his dead master's body as if he had no knowledge of what he had done. He had reverted to his docile self, now crying for his loss. Emma Cavendish took the warm lifeless body by the feet and dragged it through the opening and around to the back of the old farm building. The remnants of an old well were still there, unused now for generations. Clumps of weed were growing out of the stonework, making it unrecognisable as a source of water. But the shaft was still there, dark and very deep.

* * *

For the entire day, Phil Keane had avoided going near the prison cell where he had seen or thought he had seen the ghost of Jamey Cronin. It was almost eight in the evening and his colleague had already left for home. Relieved that the day was over, Phil locked up and left. It was cool as he walked along the shaded lane at the side of the Garda station. A few minutes and he was home, if you could call it a home.

This was always the worse part of the day for Phil; when he turned the key in the lock and pushed his front door open to step into the entrance hall where everything was always the same, lifeless, just as he had left it. No one had been there to tidy things. No one had moved the jacket which he had left slung over the end of the banister. The post and junk mail lay forlorn on the mat by the front door. He had become untidy since Mary died. There seemed little purpose in keeping the place in good order. His face reddened as he stooped to pick up the post. He carried the letters into the living room where he slung them on the coffee table. He slumped into his armchair and flicked the television into life. He kept a bottle of whiskey and a cutglass tumbler on the coffee table. He poured his usual shot and settled into the monotony of whatever came on the television. screen.

An hour or so later and for the want of something to do or for a bit of company, Phil decided to walk over to the Shamrock Hotel for a pint. He pulled a cardigan over his blue policeman's shirt and ran a comb through his thinning silvery hair. It was then that he realised that he had left his wallet in the drawer of his desk at the station. He debated with himself as to whether he should forget it, have a cup of tea and go to bed. *Local cop afraid of ghosts, he joked to himself ... No way.*

The streetlights made morbid shadows as Phil almost marched along the lane and across the front of the Garda station towards the main door. He slid the key into the lock and pushed the door open. He stepped inside. The heavy outer door closed, masking a clamour which echoed through the deserted building. He flicked the switch and the light in the foyer came on. Nervously, he whistled, almost running into his office and grabbing his wallet which he had left in the open top drawer of the desk. Phil was at the main entrance door again now, pulling at it, desperately pulling at the handle, but it just wouldn't budge. He knew he hadn't locked it, but he tried the key anyway. It still wouldn't open. He leaned his back against the door. Ridiculous, he thought, calm down, Phil Keane. This is stupid. He tried the door handle once more but nothing. It was dead in his hand. He went back into the office but the bars on the outside of the windows prevented him from escaping there too. Phil was panicking now. The fear was crushing him as he looked around the office of the Garda station. Then he froze and stared at what was appearing before him. It was the ghost of Jamey Cronin. He grabbed the phone, frantically dialling the home number of his colleague but the line was dead, a frustrating doomed silence on the receiver.

The howling noise came like some demented beast as the files on the desk moved. They were on the floor now, a scattered mess of papers. The awful noise rammed into his head as anything that could move, moved. Pictures and charts flew off the walls as if they were being torn off by an invisible gang of vandals. The desk was tossed over like a boat caught in a tempest. Phil was shaking with fear. Now there were faces around him. He ran through to the foyer and up the stairs. The faces followed him as he ran to the end of the landing. Now the faces were before him, laughing, screaming with the anguish of murdered souls. And among the faces, Jamey Cronin appeared, moving towards him. Phil watched in terror as the ghoulish figure displayed a ripped bedsheet in the form of a hangman's noose. Phil was at the top of the stairs again, then suddenly he was falling through the air, tumbling, tumbling, falling. His head hit the floor with an almighty whack, and everything went silent.

None of the clientele or staff across the street in the Shamrock Hotel could have guessed that Sergeant Phil Keane, the village Garda for the past thirty odd years, lay dead at the bottom of the Garda Station stairs. His blood had formed a pool around his head and his open eyes showed the terror of his last moments.

* * *

Earlier that evening, George had showered, shaved and pulled on a shirt, jeans and a jacket. Father Casey's bottle of holy water bulked awkwardly in the jacket pocket. He didn't feel afraid and that perplexed him a little. After all, according to Father Casey, he was about to meet an evil supernatural force. George had never given the subject much thought before. Now it seemed that he was in the thick of it or about to go into the thick of it. Even though a part of him wanted to jump into the car and drive away from this nightmare village, there was also a part telling him to stay but he couldn't understand what or why, but then perhaps he could … something in the very back of his mind. Normally, he relied on his fight or flight instincts, invariably giving in to his survival impulses. He consoled himself with the thought that deep down he didn't believe in all that rubbish as portrayed by Father Casey and besides, Emma Cavendish was a very beautiful woman, and he wasn't going to let a load of religious nonsense get in the way of him having a good time. Nevertheless, George Murray, an intelligent, rational businessman from Dublin opened the bottle of holy water, shook a few drops into the palm of his hand and daubed it onto his face as if it were an aftershave.

George was relieved to see Thwaites's Land Rover parked in the driveway next to the Mercedes. One other car sat in the shade beneath the rhododendron tree, giving him further confidence that with other people around, nothing untoward would happen. Sammy came to greet him, showing no hint of his brutal behaviour of earlier that day. Other than Sammy, there was no sign of life as George's footsteps crunched across the gravel towards the conservatory. He went in by the swimming pool towards the door which led into the house. He felt a little foolish as the door opened suddenly just as he was poised to push against it.

"Hello lover." Said Emma, thrusting her face forward to be kissed.

George obliged, tasting the fresh minty flavour on her lips. She looked hippy, her hair tossed in strange looking tufts and wisps. He wasn't sure whether it was deliberate or if she just hadn't bothered to comb it. Her red painted toenails with tanned feet peeped out from beneath a loosely fitting floral dress while dangly earrings brushed against the sides of her neck. Emma reached out, taking George by the hand and led him through to the lounge.

The curtains in the lounge were drawn and the flames of a half dozen or so candles, fused into an intoxicating glow. A redolence of smouldering joss sticks filled the air in the room while exotic oriental music played in the background. He could see the faces of shadowy figures who were lounging on the armchairs and couches. George's gaze was taken by the painting of the Full Moon which hung over the fireplace. The Moon in the painting seemed to draw in and emit light as if it had been designed to do both; hypnotic but inspiring, on the cusp between two creators.

"Everyone! This is my friend George." Emma said.

George looked at the faces, acknowledging with polite nods, the succession of *hellos* and indifferent smiles. A young couple lounged on various parts of each other. A middle-aged man sat on one of the armchairs being spoon fed by a much younger girl who had hair down to her hips. Two young men sat together on the floor.

"Drink?" Said Emma.

George smiled. "Please."

They all seemed harmless enough. George thought. Any fears about being offered up as a satanic sacrifice were gradually leaving his mind. *Just a dope party ... Never been to a real dope party before. Might as well indulge and enjoy it all. Besides, Thwaites is bound to be close by.*

Emma put a goblet to George's lips. He drank from the goblet as if he hadn't a care in the world. Gracefully, Emma sat onto a large cushion on the floor. With a slightly aging groan, George sat on a cushion next to her. One of the young boys passed a reefer to Emma. She took her drag and put it to George's lips.

"Good stuff." She said, snuggling close to him. "You'll like it."

George wasn't going to refuse, reminding himself of the old saying that it is better to live for one day as a lion rather than a thousand days as a sheep. He took the reefer, drawing the smoke back into his lungs. He passed the reefer on to the eager next person then he took another drink from the goblet.

"Oh, I forgot. You like cigars." Said Emma, as she reached for a box on a nearby coffee table.

Emma took a cigar from the box and lit it with a candle, sending a pall of smoke across George's face. She handed the cigar to him then took one for herself. With the humming and droning of the music, Emma sat there sending smoke rings into the candle-lit room. Two pairs of bare feet were sticking out from behind a long sofa. The couple on the sofa were entwined like an Adam and Eve waxwork. A few words floated here and there through the air. The mesmerising music with the drink, whatever that was, and the smoking were having their combined effect. George was sinking into a deep relax. Father Casey's warnings just didn't matter now.

The room was spinning, slowly at first, then faster and faster like some whirlwind of colours, a giant kaleidoscope. The colours melted away and reappeared as a jumbled mess. The other guests appeared through the colours but now they had changed, altered in some way or taken apart and reassembled in a clown's workshop. The middle-aged man became a middle-aged woman but was still wearing his own clothes. His young lady companion became a handsome young man, an Adonis in a dress. The two young men on the floor became two young women in men's clothes and the couple on the sofa became each other but still wearing their own clothes.

George gave a scratch to his left ear. Something dangled from it, an earring. He touched his other ear. There was an earring there too. He was quite amused by this, accepting whatever was happening to him or whatever he imagined was happening to him. A light draft hit him just above his ankles. He stretched his hand to feel his bare shin beneath the hem of a dress. He was wearing Emma's dress. He turned to her, giggling like a schoolgirl. He was looking at himself or was he Emma. He didn't really know. He didn't really care. He had her body so she could have his, trying a new fashion. This philosophy of swapping bodies and even souls seemed to be quite in order.

"So, what's it like to kiss me?" He said, his voice; sleepy.

"You can find that out for yourself." He heard Emma say or was it he himself who said that, but the words did come from Emma's mouth.

He giggled stupidly, sucking on his cigar. There was weightiness or some sort of encumbrance around his chest. Exploring his new breasts, he caught Emma's eye and they stared at each other for a while or was it for an eternity? George didn't care. Her eyes were like two mini crystal balls as if a film were being played, his own little cinema. Suddenly he was in there, in the film, a child again, playing on the dirt floor among the jagged white crumbling walls of the *Alamo*. Emma's eyes became those of the Tinker girl. George was there, his hand on her breasts, feeling, groping. That funny tingling sensation came to his lower stomach and groin area; making him want to need her, to hold her close and tight as if to become one with her. He could see her, taste her, smell her. It was as if time itself had stopped with him and he was staring into a destiny with the Tinker girl. Then he saw her ugly rage as she pointed angrily at him with her ghostly outstretched arm, demanding payment for what he had taken, demanding her money.

Then came the curse with that awful screeching banshee wail, echoing around the walls of the *Alamo*. "Beware the Blue Moon."

He saw the faces of his pals, Alfie and Pete. Alfie as a little boy, shy, always agreeing, following the pack. Then he saw

Alfie as a young man. It was as if a video were playing. Then George saw Alfie as a drunk, a depressed ragged man with no faith in himself and no hope. He saw the broken man with his spirit sinking in a sea of overwhelming inner torment. He saw Alfie looking into water, glossy still water, reflecting the Full Moon. The Moon was laughing at him and then it became Alfie's own face. Alfie was the Man in the Moon. It beckoned, seeming to be his friend, reaching out to welcome him. George saw Alfie the man, as he surrendered to the friendly face shimmering on the water and then Alfie slipped beneath the surface and was gone.

In his mind, George was petrified, his limbs seized in their sockets as if he was in a straitjacket. He tried to put his hand to his face but there was no movement from the uncooperative limb. He tried to close his eyes, but they were stuck open, forcing him to watch his own horrific nightmare. Worst of all, he was unable to call out. He wanted so desperately to scream but nothing came. He was trapped, trapped on a conveyor belt to hell.

The terror rolled on. Old Meg came into his mind. Old Meg, the country simpleton he had so often called cruel names when he was a boy. That poor lonely old bird whose heart and soul had died long before her body did. Now George had his own front seat from which to view old Meg's tormented last hour on this earth. He saw the Full Moon beckoning her, throwing its silvery light across the meadow and over the haunting walls of the *Alamo*. He watched, captive, as she went through the meadow, her white wedding dress, glowing in the moonlight. George wanted to help her, to warn her and to get her away from that evil place. But he couldn't move, couldn't reach out, couldn't pull her back. He could see what Meg had seen as if he were in her mind, looking out through her eyes. Then he was looking at the noose as it hung over the lintel. The noose turned into the Full Moon and then it turned into an image of George's own face. Now, he watched himself being part of the evil, as if the good Christian George was observing his own satanic opposite.

The horrendous *reality* continued. The film changed as if someone had flicked a remote control and suddenly, he was in St Kevin's. Mother Antonia was coming towards him, her black habit concealing the movements of her limbs as she seemed to glide over the polished floor. George felt safe now, safe amid the kindly, god-fearing nuns who devoted their lives to Christ and to mankind. Mother Antonia's head was bent forward, her face hidden in her veil. She looked up but her face was the Moon, an ugly sneering moon. It was as if the Mother Superior was playing some terrible cruel trick; an agent of Christ revealing herself to be an agent of the Antichrist. More nuns appeared, all wearing the same mocking countenance, all sneering, all closing in on him. The nightmare went on.

Pete suddenly appeared. He had a Rosary wound around his fist with the crucifix held high, defying the demon nuns. Pete had come to rescue his old pal. He moved bravely towards the moon-faces, making them draw back, making them squirm as the symbol of good struck fear into them. Pete moved forward, chanting the Hail Mary as he did. He stood before George and then the cruel trick was played once more. The crucifix in Pete's hand became the Moon and it too sneered and laughed at George and he could only watch as the chanting baying mob closed in to claim him.

As the odious mob was about to kill, the picture changed again. George was still unable to move or even protest at these petrifying scenes. He was trying to wake from this awful nightmare, but he was unable. He could see himself with Lisa in her little red car. He pulled the sun visor down to see his own face in the mirror. Horror struck him again as the Moon grinned back at him as if more dark mischief were about to happen. He saw himself grabbing the steering wheel, locking the car in a violent thrust to the left and sending it crashing into a wall. George saw himself leaving the wreckage and looking back for a moment to admire his handiwork. He was grinning at the decapitated body of his girlfriend and then he vanished back into the underworld.

He felt like he was going to explode. Every vein in his body seemed to be at boiling point as he watched helpless, unable to move or shout. He was confused now. Was he on the side of good or had he really stepped across some moral void and was now on the side of evil? Perhaps he was merely an observer or was he some unfortunate victim.

The colours came again. This time they had formed into a proper rainbow. The oriental music was grinding into his head; loud intense. Then he was falling, falling, falling sideways through a long dark shaft, a shaft without end, tumbling, tumbling, tumbling through the depths of time.

* * *

It was dark, completely dark and quiet. George was lying on a bed, but he had no idea as to where he was. The dream or nightmare or whatever the hell it was, had finished. Now he was in control of his thoughts again. His eyes were wide open, but he could see nothing. He sniffed the air, a damp, musty smell.

George's right arm jolted tight as he went to move it. Both arms were stretched out, tied to the frame of the bed or whatever it was he was lying on. His legs were bound also, both ankles tied to the frame. For a moment he made no attempt to struggle. He lay there, calmly accepting whatever was happening to him. A few moments passed before he realised the seriousness of his situation. Then the fear came over him. What the hell was going on, he wondered, and how did he get to be where he was? And why was he tied up? Was he a prisoner? Was this one of Emma's kinky games, part of the orgy? But why was he still wearing his clothes? He thought that this must be some practical joke or else he was in deep trouble.

He lay still, trying to compose himself. Whoever had tied him to the bed probably wouldn't know that he was awake. He thought it best that he should remain silent and keep any little advantage that he might have. Maybe Father Casey was right, and Emma Cavendish and her friends did practice the dark arts. He did not want to have anything to do with any of that kind of stuff. *No… Stay silent, stay calm.*

George pulled at the cords which tied his hands to the bed frame but the more he did, the tighter they bit into his wrists. It didn't seem to be so dark now and he could just about make out the outlines of things in the room. His arms ached. He was unable to move up or down very much. He stretched his right hand to grip one of the bars of the head frame. There was some give in the frame as it moved ever so slightly in its socket. His face, body and limbs contorted as he strained to twist the bar. No good. It wouldn't budge that way. He relaxed for a moment, his lungs drawing in more of the musty, stale air. Then he tried to slide the bar upwards and downwards in its socket. It budged a fraction and then he pulled it sideways, this time getting just a little more movement. With each jolt, he pulled down with as much strength as he could grind from his face, through his shoulders and arms and up through to his hands. Then the bar stuck as if it had been jerked out of its home. George relaxed for a moment, took a deep breath and with one almighty wrench, the bar snapped out of its socket.

Relief overcame his exhaustion. He reached over to the knot that tied his other hand. The knot was tight; his fingers probing in the dark as they traced the curves and loops of the knot. It seemed like ages before he managed to undo it but eventually it came loose, freeing his left hand.

George sat up on the bed, rubbing his wrists. Again, he had to fumble about in the dark, feeling the ropes around his ankles. His shoes were still on, suggesting that he might have walked to his prison himself. *Don't think I was dragged here*, he thought. He felt his jacket pocket. The small bottle of holy water was still there. He had a box of matches in the other pocket. He struck a match, its sulphurous whiff sweetening the stale air.

The dim yellow flame glowed warm above his fingertips, allowing him to see his surroundings properly. He was in a room of about twelve feet by twelve. A flat metal bar sat in its brackets across the window shutters, keeping them locked from any outside intrusions. There was a light switch on the wall beside the door, but he didn't want to risk drawing attention by switching it on. He blew the flame away before it had a chance to burn his fingertips.

In the dark again, he stood up from the bed and fumbled his way across the room towards the door. The knob turned dead in his hand. *Shit*, he mumbled. *What the hell are they up to and where the hell was Thwaites?* His hand felt along the damp wall until he was at the window, and he found the flat metal bar which sat across the shutters. The bar slid easily in a rotating motion and carefully, he let it hang vertically. The shutters fell open, just enough to let the grey light of the

Moon to ghost through. He pushed the shutters gently to open a little wider so he could see out into the night. Through the cobwebs and the dust and grime, he could just make out the *Alamo* in the middle distance as it peered through the darkened clumps of foliage to catch the moonlight.

George could see his surroundings better now. He guessed he was in the basement at Caqueux House. He remembered Emma saying that she didn't have a key to these rooms. An old trunk or chest of some sort prevented him from getting close to the window. He pulled it away, trying to make as little noise as possible, he opened the trunk. There were some old newspapers and a framed photograph. George held the photograph up to the moonlight. It was of a couple on their wedding day. He lit another match and held it to the picture for a few seconds. It could have been any couple on their wedding day. He was puzzled but nothing really surprised him now. The match burned out, so he lit another and held it to the photograph again. Then he remembered. It must have been old Meg.

The drug trip came back to him. The dress in the photograph was the same as the one he had seen in the nightmare; the dress that old Meg was wearing as she went across the meadow towards the *Alamo*. Old Meg, he thought. She was in his nightmare and now here she was staring out of a photograph at him. Then he thought of Josh Cogan and more memories came to him and he guessed that this had been old Meg's room. This was her room, her own room; the place about which he and his pals so often conjured up puerile images, making crude jokes … *She kidnaps children and locks them in a room beneath Josh Cogan's house. If she captures you then you are a goner, forever and ever …* But in reality, this was poor old Meg's retreat from the world; the room where she could be alone with her grief and her memories and her sad dreams of what might have been.

George searched further into the chest. He pulled out a blanket of some sort and when he held it up to the moonlight, he could see that it was a shawl. He lit another match to see the shawl properly. It was a patchwork of colours. Must have belonged to a Tinker, he thought. Then he thought of the Tinker girl in the *Alamo*, all those years ago.

He searched the chest again and found another shawl. This one had been bundled into a roll. As he unrolled it, long sticks fell out. He picked one of the sticks from the floor and looked at it under the moonlight. It was an arrow, complete with a tip and flights. But they seemed light, toy-like, maybe a boy's toy arrows. He was pondering this, wondering why someone had bothered to wrap a few old toy arrows in an old shawl and keep them in the bottom of an old trunk. Then it came to him, a memory from way back. It was Pete's special penknife. He and Alfie were so jealous of Pete for having that penknife. He sharpened the arrows with it. But these couldn't possibly be those same arrows? Sure, that was all more than thirty years before. And if they were indeed those same arrows then why on earth would anyone want to keep them and put them away carefully like this? He remembered stalking through the woods with his pals and spying on the Tinker's caravan. Then he remembered the Tinker girl who wanted money for a feel of her breasts. The girl's face was clear in his mind. He remembered thinking of how beautiful she was. But what was happening now? He wondered. Did that Tinker girl have something to do with this? Her haunting curse rang through his ears. "Beware the Blue Moon." He looked through the window. *Yes*, he thought *a Blue Moon*, and there it was, complete and full, round and bright and now menacing too and sitting right over the *Alamo* and laughing at him, and deep down in his heart and in his mind, he knew why, he knew very well why.

George dropped the arrows into the old chest and closed the lid. He pushed at the grimy catch on the window and managed to make it slide back. Cobwebs and grime covered the window frames. He strained as he tried to slide the bottom half of the window upwards, but it seemed to be stuck solid. The sash cords had stiffened, and the timbers had swollen with the dampness. There was nothing in the room that he might use to shift it. Again, he put his fingers into the brass rings at the bottom of the window, pulling and willing with his strained face and arms to move the window, even an inch. His willpower won and the window moved upwards, just by an inch or so, but it was enough for George to get his hands beneath it and then he was able to put in a good strong effort and it opened enough for him to climb through.

He scrambled up the embankment to the lawn. The cool night air was refreshing as he went along the edge of the grass. Like a stalking cat, he crept through the shadows of trees and shrubs which stood silent in the silvery light. It was as if the Moon and even Caqueux House were watching him. He peered, from the shadow of a tree along the gravelled sweep at the front of the house. The visiting car was still there, as was Thwaites's Land Rover and the yellow Mercedes, looking as if it was standing guard over his own car. He felt in his jacket pockets for the keys, but they were not there, so he was going to have to make a run for it. He looked around again, fearing that at any moment, the mad Emma Cavendish and her doped-up friends would come rushing out to capture him again and make some gruesome ritual sacrifice of him.

George sprinted along the grass verge of the driveway and was quickly past the entrance and heading towards Ballynamarbh. The quiet country road was almost equally divided along the middle, one side in the night shadow of trees and hedges, the other side, visible under the moonlight. George was running now like he hadn't run for ages, not since his last game of rugby about five years before. He had to stop for a moment to catch his breath and to nurse a sharp pain in his side, being reminded of what a stitch felt like. He remembered all the times he had to run from Josh Cogan or some other annoyed farmer or orchard owner, when he was a kid, messing about with his pals and generally living an adventurous boyhood. He thought he heard a car approaching so he hid behind a tree. Nothing appeared so he continued on his way. What had earlier seemed to be only a short distance by car now seemed like miles.

The exertion of running made him feel sick. He stopped again; his chest muscles convulsing to vomit sour bile. He wiped his face with his hanky and began to trot again. As he went, he was thinking about all the things that had happened to him over the past few days.

A sudden cold wetness engulfed him as if he had stepped into a mist. His face became cold in contrast to the sweatiness of his body after the running. The old railway bridge loomed out of the misty night, dark and silent. It seemed to hulk over him, a monument to the labours and pains of people of generations ago; all long dead now, passed over into the next world but maybe their souls were still there guarding the bridge, the bridge they built by their own sweat, with their own hands. A car was parked beside the bridge by the path which led up the side of the embankment. He could just about make out the registration number which stopped him dead. He checked it again and tried to make out the colour of the car. Lisa! Her name flew off his lips. The car wasn't parked. It had been crashed and abandoned. The bonnet was crumpled, and the windscreen was a shattered cobweb of glass with a jagged, gaping hole at the driver's side. Now he was worried about Lisa, wondering what had happened to her. There was nobody in the crashed car.

As George stood looking over the wreck, he remembered his dream or his *trip* or whatever it was. Had he foreseen this? He wondered. What was going on? What was happening to him? He shivered. But where was Lisa? Whatever had happened between him and Lisa, he certainly didn't wish her any harm. Besides, he still thought about her almost all the time. He shivered at the thought of anything awful happening to her and then the Tinker girl's curse came to him again; *beware the Blue Moon.*

Ballynamarbh was quiet, very quiet, too quiet. The mist had settled over the entire village now and it seemed to contain the light from the streetlamps, all lined up like a platoon of yellow clad sentries who had nodded off during their watch. Parked cars kept a dumb kerbside vigil. Darkened windows spied morbidly, refusing any kind of succour. Everywhere was lifeless, wrapped in a deadening mist of grey diffused moonlight.

The Garda station door stared back at George, his anxious knocking going unheard, and little did he know that Sergeant Phil Keane's body lay dead at the bottom of the stairs on the other side of the door.

He went across the street to the Shamrock Hotel. Safety, he thought. But the doors there too were locked; the tourists sleeping soundly in their beds. Where was the night porter? George could hear the bell ringing through the foyer on the other side of the door, but it made no difference. The gates at the back entrance to the hotel had been drawn together and locked tight with a hefty padlock. George ran to the middle of the street; the broken white lines on the road zipping away from him in either direction into the cold night mist.

He ran up to the church. He would be safe there. Father Casey was sure to be there. He was wet now. A film of cold droplets covered his jacket and the dampness seemed to be clinging to him like a clammy handshake. He consciously refused to look at the old churchyard as he hurried by the side of the church towards the presbytery. Father Casey's car wasn't there. It was usually parked by the door but now it was uncomfortably absent. A porch light shone a grudging welcome. He rang the bell, giving it a long, distressed press. A few seconds seemed like minutes but there was no answer. He pushed it again, hearing it resonate on the inside. Again, he waited, shuffling anxiously on his feet. But still. no answer.

George ran back past the church which, from the outside, appeared to be in darkness. He ran through the old church yard and out onto the top of the village street. What the hell was going on? He wondered. Was this all some bad dream? He was distressed and half exhausted now, wanting to rest. But where was Lisa? Where was Father Casey and where were the Gardaí? Surely the whole village hadn't just packed up and gone away? Surely, they weren't all in such a deep sleep that not one single person could be roused.

A shadowy figure appeared in the distance at the bottom of the street down towards the old railway bridge. Lisa, he thought, wishfully. He called her name, but the figure vanished into the mist. He ran towards the bridge, the downward slope making the run easy for him. He called out again: *Lisa, Lisa* as he looked for the face he knew so well. Now he was beside the crashed car again but there wasn't anyone there.

There was no mist beyond the old railway bridge, only the Moon glowing eerily in an inky sky, throwing its ghostly light over the land while drawing silhouetted outlines along the hedgerows. George looked up at the embankment, thinking that he saw a shadow or something, somewhere up there. He ran along the path and was soon on the disused railway line. If it was Lisa then he had to stop her, stop her from going towards the *Alamo,* or the woods, or anywhere near Caqueux. Perhaps she was injured, concussed or something worse or desperately confused, desperately seeking help?

* * *

Father Casey did not hear George ringing the doorbell because he wasn't in the presbytery. He was alone in the church. He had been there for a while, taking a blessing with holy water to every corner of the building. Earlier, he had rested and then he had prepared himself like some general on the eve of a great battle. Now, he knelt at the altar, not facing it but with his back to it. He was on guard. Candles, arranged in the shape of the cross, flickered on the floor before him. Bowls of holy water sat within reach of his hands and a crucifix hung from his neck.

The priest's loud prayers chanted around the vaulted building as he concentrated on each slow, distinct word, invoking the help of Christ and the support of the Virgin Mary, asking for strength and courage in his imminent battle against the grotesque evil that he knew was about to attack him. The moonlight sharpened the image of Saint Patrick on one of the stained-glass windows. Father Casey lost his concentration for a moment as he gazed at the image of Ireland's patron saint banishing snakes from the land.

Not long now, he thought, knowing that they would come at any time after midnight with the Full Moon high in the sky. Sweat beads formed on his forehead and he could feel the wetness around his already uncomfortable Roman collar. He was chanting faster determinedly now as if stopping would give the enemy an advantage. The glowing light from the array of candles around him faded into the darkness at the back of the church.

He remembered the accounts of the other priests who had witnessed what he was about to see. He wondered why he had not yet been struck down like the others. Why he wasn't dead or worse like poor old Father Pete, a bewildered idiot. He prayed for George Murray, knowing that there was a reason for his showing up in Ballynamarbh at this time and a particular reason why George had those apparitions. But what those reasons were, Father Casey just did not know. He was thinking that this whole gory episode might just be a crazy hysteria on his part and maybe if he didn't recognise these happenings or manifestations or whatever they were, then they might just go away or might not even exist at all. This doubting made him feel stronger as if defying the enemy to even exist. He remonstrated with himself for letting his mind drift. Keep focused, he told himself, keep praying, and keep invoking Christ.

The low moaning sound came, like that of some maddened beast in the distance. But Father Casey knew that this was no animal. No, this was the audible grief of the dead or rather the half dead. It came for a second or two then stopped, a threatening silence. It came again, louder this time before tapering off again. As he prayed, Father Casey peered into the darkness. Then something happened that he hadn't seen before. At the back of the church a figure emerged from near the confession box. The figure grew brighter as if a light was glowing within it. It was a girl. She stood there for a moment, still, motionless, staring. Father Casey prayed louder, watching as the girl turned away from him and moved towards the main doors at the very back of the church. A heavy clunking noise echoed throughout the church as the bolts on the doors slid back and then the big wooden doors flew open accompanied by a howling gust of wind as it blasted its way into the building.

Then he heard them; the now familiar moans of men at first, then the wailing of the women, that shrill banshee wail that only women can make and then the screaming of the children. It was all like some horrifying opera warning of Armageddon, with the rabble on the march.

Father Casey prayed louder, harder, faster. He could feel their presence now as he tried desperately to stop their advance with his concentrated prayers, pleading to Christ. He was trembling with fear as he felt their anger which in their half-death had turned to hatred and to evil. Then he saw them, faint at first, just the outlines of their faces and bodies; the darkened figures of men, women and children; all marching out of some occulted time pocket.

On his knees, he prayed harder, tightening his hands around the crucifix, if that were possible. They kept coming; gaunt, ghostly faces whose eyes were invisible in the dark recesses of their skulls and their emaciated bodies clothed in rags. He wanted to stop praying and reason with them but how could he reason with ghosts. How could anyone reason with those who were under the control of the satanic forces? Perhaps they might change, he thought. Perhaps there was still some good in them. No, he remonstrated with himself, this is evil here, evil coming out into the open, showing its ugly face in the form of death and anger and hatred. No, he thought, this is a war and right now he was on the front line, and he was outnumbered.

They were near the altar now. He could smell them as the air around him filled with the putrid stench of rotting flesh and the moaning of the tormented souls wailed through the air, ripping at his ears and through his head like a jagged blade. The unsettled dead stopped before the altar where only a few days before he had performed a wedding ceremony for a young couple; a wedding ceremony when everyone had been at their happiest and when he, for a while at least, enjoyed performing his normal pastoral duties.

Father Casey stretched his hand into the nearest bowl of holy water and shook it forward, sprinkling the area before him. The deafening sounds were all around him now, closing in on him, directing their evil towards him with their zombie faces. The clamouring noise, the putrid smell and the intense evil stabbed violently at him, every part of him. He could hear his heart pounding away inside his chest and he felt that he might explode. He knew all about these shouts and screams. He had spent the previous years gathering information about the massacre of the innocent, the wretched French Caqueux family. He had learnt all about the atrocity that had been perpetrated some two hundred years before on the very site where he now knelt and prayed. It was a night when the Moon was full and the second Full Moon of that month; a Blue Moon. Whenever there was a Blue Moon, the Caqueux family would arrive. They would come, faint at first; whispers becoming louder as they marched to the sacred place where they once thought they would be safe.

Now they were coming; full strength, out of their Limbo, filled with rage and torment and seeking vengeance. They wanted their revenge on this place of Christ, the place where they had run for safety, claiming sanctuary from the marauding mob that wanted to kill them. But they were not safe there. They had been chased to the Christian God's house and then murdered by hunters who pulled the children from their mothers, hacking, slashing, murdering. Anyone who managed to escape to the fields were hunted down like animals and destroyed as if they had some terrible disease. And all the while, the priest looked away, unwilling or unable to interfere, unwilling to stand up to the mob and protect those who came to his church for sanctuary.

Now they were marching towards Father Casey, just as they had marched on Father Philpott when the spirits of the Caqueux were aroused on the killing of another Gipsy girl: Anna Louise Caddy. Her restless spirit had never left Ballynamarbh or the farm that once belonged to Josh Cogan. In death she had joined the war with her ancestors as they sought vengeance against the descendants and the successors of those who persecuted them.

The stench of death was pungent, choking. Father Casey was weakening as the leering wailing faces closed in. He prayed harder, louder, holding his crucifix before them, showing it to the faces of the souls who were unable to find peace. Then the image of Father Philpott appeared, kneeling beside him, facing the onslaught. Then more images appeared, kneeling beside Father Casey, images of long dead priests who had also served at St Vincent's, some of whom had had first-hand experience of the restless, vengeful souls of the wretched French Gipsies.

The ghostly images of the priests knelt beside Father Casey, giving their support to the present holder of their office against the forces of evil who wanted to take this holy place for their own master. The chanting of the priests was being drowned out by the moans and the wailing of the dead. Then a demented cry wailed over the altar behind them

.... *"Sanctuaire .... Asile .... Les enfants .... Asile"*.....

Candle flames flickered dementedly under the angry wind that whipped about the Altar. Father Casey dipped his fingers into the holy water again, flicking it wildly with a blessing motion. But as he did, some drops fell on a candle flame which flared up as if it the holy water had turned into petrol. Other drops turned to a blood red as they fell on the white marble steps to the altar.

Father Casey feared that he was losing this battle. Then his hand which had touched the holy water was engulfed in the fire and the flames shot with terrifying speed along his sleeve. The wind turned to a gale and the doors at the back of the church slammed with a loud distressing echo thumping throughout the building. The flames had engulfed Father Casey now. The human torch stumbled to his feet for a few moments then fell on the red strip of carpet that lay the length of the aisle between the altar and the back of the church. The faces of the dead moaned louder as the gale spread the flames along the carpet and into the pews where generations of the good people of Ballynamarbh had worshipped.

* * *

The still, glassy waters of the lake reflected a perfect Moon. It was quiet here with no mist, unlike the village street or the vengeful destruction at St Vincent's. George had been running for some time. He was trying to catch up with Lisa. He had to stop her. It was as if he was on automatic now, not really thinking clearly. He had only thought that he had seen Lisa, but his mind had convinced him that it really was her.

Dark shadows seemed to move in the distance. Rabbits, rats, he told himself. He stumbled but just about managed to stay on his feet and as he ran, his mind raced too. The drink, the dope or whatever the hell it was that the mad Emma had given him along with all the other weird things that had happened to him since his arrival in Ballynamarbh, were combining to make him feel weird and sick again. Panting, he slumped against a tree and between his gasps of exhaustion his eyes focussed back to the village where a patch on the dark horizon glowed red. He regarded the scene for a moment. But he couldn't have known that what he was seeing in the distant night was the inferno that now raged at St Vincent's where the flames had spread through the pews and the confession boxes and now the roof itself was ablaze. He couldn't have heard the vengeful ghostly mob, wailing like a thousand banshees with their evil, burning, howling, taking hold as if it was already a hell and where Father Casey's cindered body lay engulfed in the flames with the crucifix buried in his charred fist; the crucifix that hadn't protected him, for that night victory went to the other side.

George was running again. His muscles were aching, his chest, gasping for air. His only concern now was to stop Lisa from falling into the clutches of whatever evil it was that possessed the land around Caqueux House.

There she was again, a nebulous figure moving away from him in the distance. His eyes followed the moving patch of brightness then it fled into the woods. George cut off along a rut through the scrub, following what he thought to be Lisa.

It was darker now in the woods, much darker with only glints of silvery moonlight spying through the treetops. He could hear his own footsteps as withered leaves and pieces of broken branches crunched under his weight. A sudden jerk tore along his right arm as he went past the jagged stump of a branch. He tripped or was it something or someone had tripped him. Did something reach out of the darkness to grab him? His mind played. The ground was wet and soggy as his hands flattened to break the sudden fall. For a few seconds he stayed on the ground, exhausted with the earthy smell of lush growth streaming up his nostrils. He scrambled back to his feet and moved on, stumbling here and there, afraid to look back.

Gasping for breath, George slumped to a crouch by the foot of some large tree. The smooth knotty buttress comforted him for a moment. The thought went through his head as to what on earth he was doing. What the hell was going on? Was he out of his mind altogether? His head slumped and his own warm sweaty, sweet body odour seeped up from the inside of his jacket. He could have been slumped by that tree for a few minutes or for a good while longer. He didn't really know, and he was beginning not to care. He felt exhausted and beaten. The fear, along with the mind-bending events of the previous few hours were crushing him.

A glinting through the trees grew brighter. George pondered it for a moment and relief came over him as he realised that the grassy glade was there before him. From there he would be able to get his bearings and he would go back to the village for help to find Lisa.

George pulled himself up to a stand then went forward under the sporadic light of the moon. His clothes felt damp and sticky. His chest hurt and his face was sore; swelling from the lacerations he'd received from rushing through branches and briars. He was at the edge of the glade, his hand resting on a tree trunk for support. His eyes peered and his jaw dropped as he looked with astonishment at the sight before him. The moonlight shone like a theatre spotlight, pointing out the very centre of the glade. He stayed where he was for a moment before slowly stepping forward. He took a few more steps with the moonlight showing the way and then he stood still again.

He stood there, staring at the bizarre scene. A silent procession of ghostly faces above their nebulous bodies filed out from between the trees at the far side of the glade. He could only gaze dumbstruck at the surreal sight. The tormented souls, who had finally had their revenge on St Vincent's church, were returning to their mass grave where, nearly two centuries before, their murdered bodies had been callously buried, dumped, hidden. George watched as they formed a circle, ghosts of adults and children, discernible only by their heights. They joined, as if holding hands, and stood for a moment, all aglow in a mist like some biblical vision and then they seemed to vanish into the ground.

The night air was silent, otherworldly. Low, distant, animal sounds reassured George that he was still in his own world. Some distant dog barked a lonely far off echo. Otherwise, George Murray was alone with his nightmare.

His mind was still ticking over. He thought of what Father Casey had told him about the French Gipsies. How they had been chased and slaughtered. How they fled, in fear of their lives, across the fields, before they were brutally sent to their deaths and how the whole event had been dismissed as *only a myth* by the locals ever since. Nobody had ever known or would admit to knowing where exactly the poor wretches had been buried and it was all too easy for the good people of Ballynamarbh to deny that those horrific events ever took place. The half dead had had their revenge and had retreated to their mass grave where they might finally rest in peace and George could not have known about the horrible events in St Vincent's and at the Garda station. A tranquillity came over him on seeing the ghostly figures as they retreated into their earthy resting place. It was as if a wrong had been righted. He felt a little better now as his breathing and heartbeat returned to normal.

A light mist covered the meadow. The grey light of dawn gave George a renewed courage. It was as if he was testing himself as he headed towards the *Alamo*. Now he wanted to purge his own ghosts, whatever or whoever they were.

* * *

The jagged walls of the *Alamo* appeared out of the dawn mist, and he went inside. A man was standing with his back to him. The man slowly turned around. It was quite clearly the face of Arthur Thwaites but with a solemn pale look about him. Thwaites was different now and George knew that he was seeing a ghost. The ghost of Thwaites spoke in a whispery way.

"It is time." Said the ghost.

George knew what the ghost meant. He knew exactly what it meant. It was indeed time, time to admit to himself what had happened all those years ago as his mind replayed the events of that last afternoon when he played with Alfie and Pete on Josh Cogan's land. He could see it clearly, like a film being played in his mind. He could see himself looking through the binoculars at the Tinker girl as she washed in the lake. How he and his pals, in their puerile state, fought over the binoculars to get a look.

Then they found it, the gun, a real pistol, just like the pistols they had seen soldiers carrying in the war films at the cinema. The pistol, he remembered, had been put in a wooden box which had been wrapped in sacking and hidden under a pile of stones on the railway embankment. As George thought about it, he guessed that the pistol might have been there since the civil war or maybe it might have been hidden there by some subversive or other or it might have been hidden there by some gangster to use when the right opportunity arose. George remembered that it was he who grabbed the pistol from the box. Now, George cursed himself for his impetuous, puerile action.

He could see it now as if it were a film running through his mind; the three of them rolling about in the undergrowth, shooting their arrows, trying to be like real Indians. A real gun was such a find, an adult thing in the hands of children. The gun's mechanism was stiff. George remembered trying to pull the trigger several times as he pretended to be John Wayne, firing at bare-chested savages. Then they were near the glade. They came together, signalling one another, like real Indians preparing for an ambush. Pete stood up and shouted .... *charge* .... and like a pack of wild dogs, they ran, marauding through the glade just as the Tinker girl was burying her dead mother. George fired the pistol but this time the trigger moved, and a shot rang out; an awful, sudden, irretrievable, damning clap that registered in his mind faster than the bullet flew to its innocent, accidental target.

The scene was vivid in George's mind now as the film in his head replayed the way he and Pete and Alfie stopped dead in their tracks. They were looking at the Tinker girl; her body slumped over the edge of the grave with a stream of blood from her head soaking into the brown earth.

"Shit."

That swear-word, which Pete uttered, resonated loudly like some time bomb in George's head. He could see the scene so clearly now even after a lifetime of supressing it. The boys looked at each other in a numbed desperation as their boyhoods left them and the reality of the world set in.

"Is she dead?" Said Pete.

Alfie just shrugged.

George was sure she was dead. There was no movement from the girl and besides with a hole like that in her head and with that amount of blood, she was better off dead.

It was as if some sort of defence or denial mechanism immediately shut down on them and they simply pushed the body into the grave where *some other body* had already been laid and with the Tinker girl's own spade, George shovelled the brown earth onto her ragdoll body. When the grave was filled with the brown earth, George patted the mound and spread the earth to make it level. The tragedy was gone, out of sight. It never happened; the terrible thing never, ever happened … One for all, and all for one…

Now a lifetime later, George stood between the *Alamo* walls thinking about what he did, all those years ago. His thoughts were clear and honest and contrite.… *Didn't even try to find out if the poor little girl was still alive …. just heaped the dirt onto her helpless body. If she was alive then what torture had I put her through? …. Oh God, what did I do …. what on earth did I do? ….*

George shivered in his guilt as he remembered how they covered the grave with leaves and briars and then how he went back to the railway embankment and how he threw the pistol into the lake. He remembered how they pushed the Tinker's caravan deeper into the woods and the undergrowth and then let the horse loose to wander wherever it would. And then they made the pact; the secret pact under pain of death that they would never, ever say anything to anyone, not even to themselves, about what had happened.

George was deep in thought. Pete had tried to make amends by going into the priesthood, but his mind couldn't take it. And Alfie, poor little Alfie who, at first, was able to make a life for himself and then it all fell apart on him. Was it some kind of karmic retribution that made Alfie's life turn so wretched that the only way out for him was to kill himself?

The ghost of Arthur Thwaites had gone. Something was catching the corner of George's eye. He half turned to find Emma Cavendish standing there. This wasn't the flirty, vivacious Emma, but a serious looking Emma as if she had something practical to do.

"You remember now?" She said.

George nodded. His face was pained with remorse. "And where do you fit into all this? Are you real or what?"

"Does it matter?" She said and paused for a moment. "But there is a way out for you."

"What do you mean; a way out?"

"I mean; you think I'm evil …. Don't you."

George shrugged. "I don't know anymore .... Tell me, what was all that about last night? .... Why? Did I really see ghosts in the glade? Did you drug me? .... Why did you lock me in the basement?"

Emma smiled. "Yes, you really did see what you call ghosts. They're at rest now. They've had their justice." Emma took a few steps forward and was now only a few feet away from George. "You do remember that you crossed that Tinker girl. You tricked her. You cheated her and then she cursed you. You do remember, don't you?"

George nodded.

"But then you killed her; an accident, but you buried her not even knowing whether she was dead or alive. Did you even know her name?"

"What was her name?" Said George.

"It was Anna Louise. You cheated her and killed her. You hid her body. All of which resonated with the restless souls of the murdered French Gipsies. Their half dead spirits identified with the great injustice that was done to her and especially because of where it happened, sacred ground. It was as if history was repeating itself."

Emma's words cut deep, and George could not deny what she was saying. He raised his chin slightly. "And you? Who exactly are you?"

"Well, you might well think that I am your conscience, but no." She said, shaking her head. "You see, you never gave any thought about the person who was already in that grave;

the person Anna Louise was laying to rest at the moment you killed her."

"Who was that person?" Said George.

"Emma raised her eyebrows slightly. "It was me. I had died and my daughter was laying me to rest. I was looking down at the scene, at my own burial which Anna Louise, my beautiful daughter had so lovingly arranged. She had no one else in the world and you came along, and you took her life. But it was the way you treated her small lifeless body is what really angered me. I could not rest after that. I knew that one day you would return."

George was taking these words in. He felt surprised that he wasn't afraid of this encounter with this supernatural being or whatever it was.

"You said there was a way out for me." Said George.

She looked at him for a long moment which made him feel to be at her mercy.

"Yes there is." She eventually said.

"And?"

"Oh I think you will have to find that inside yourself."

With a pensive downward gaze, George pondered these words. After a few moments he looked up, but Emma Cavendish wasn't there. He looked around and called out, but there was no answer. He stood alone with his thoughts amid the crumbling, jagged ruins which he and his boyhood pals once called 'the *Alamo*.'

Part Three

The stillness of the morning sat on the meadow as the sun's warmth dispersed the woolly mist that lay in pockets here and there across the land. George looked at his watch; nearly eight. He felt at peace as he walked towards Caqueux House, and a pigeon seemed to concur with a bout of low, reassuring cooing. Caqueux House looked harmless enough now as he went towards the front. There were no other cars there, except for his own car, waiting there for him; a welcome sight. A whistling gardener, pushing a wheelbarrow, appeared from near the pool-house. He settled his wheelbarrow on the gravel as George approached.

"Hello." Said the gardener. "Are ya lookin for someone?"

"Is Emma Cavendish around?" Said George.

The worker shook his head.

"You're a bit late, boye."

George was puzzled. "What do you mean?"

The old boy took a hoe which had been lying on the barrow and wedged the blade beneath a clump of weeds. "She was killed, God rest her, out there in the meadow. Was scoolin a horse. The divil, didn't he go and trow her headlong into the wall of that old building over there... killed stone dead, she was."

George thought for a moment. He wasn't surprised by anything anymore.

"Had she been living here for long?"

"Oh, she came here, a mere slip or a girl but very womanly all the same. Around the time of the big storm, way back in the sixties. She was an artist from England. Old Cogan, who owned the place at the time, he just couldn't resist her. There was a fair age difference between 'em but that didn't stop 'em. But with all her youth and good looks, she was never able to give him a child, which he wanted more than anything. Poor old Cogan drank himself into the grave .... She married agin, more wealth and she buried that poor bastard too."

"Tell me. Is Arthur Thwaites here?" Said George.

The old boy smiled. "Are you from the television?"

"No." Said George, shaking his head. "I used to live around here when I was a boy." He pulled a business card from his pocket and gave it to the old boy who inspected it with a suspicious, countryman's eye.

"Were you from down the road?" He said.

"That's right." Said George.

"Begod, I knew your father. Is he still alive?"

"Ah sure, he passed away a few years back." Said George.

"Oh, I'm sorry to hear that."

"You were saying about Thwaites." Said George.

"Ah yes. He should be here today, but I haven't seen him yet. His Land Rover isn't there so he must be off somewhere … Wasn't it awful about poor Father Casey? Didn't he die in the fire last night." Said the old boy, blessing himself."

"Fire? What fire?" Said George. Sounding anxious.

"Didn't ya hear?" Saint Vincent's was burned to the ground last night and Father Casey inside it."

George went silent for a moment, thinking about Father Casey while the old boy continued with his weeding. After another while, he spoke again.

"So, who lives in this house now?" He asked.

"Ah, 'tis vacant since the lady of the house died. We just take care of the place, meself and Arthur. We do a few odd jobs for the solicitors while they're looking for the rightful heirs."

George looked at his watch. "Well, I'd better be off. Nice to have met you."

The old boy took a car key from his pocket and held it up. "I found this on the drive. Is it yours?"

"Ah, thanks. I was looking for that."

He sat into the car and drove off

His mind was at rest as he drove back to the village. He wasn't at all shocked or even surprised at what had been uncovered about his past. It had been there all along, buried deep in his mind. He didn't doubt the reality of it all. He wasn't confused about what had happened but now George was able to see the truth. The boy playing in the *Alamo* all those years ago was like some other person, some other life, some other world, some other reality. But that boy had grown into the man and now the man had to take responsibility for the boy's actions. It was his, George Murray's, very own personal timeline from the day he was born right up until the minute he would die and once he had reached the age of reason then he had to be responsible for his own actions. He wondered if good and evil were merely perceptions. Did good and evil exist beyond the grave? He wondered.

George had to park his car at the bottom of the street by the old railway bridge as the village had been cordoned off. Uniformed Gardaí stood in silence as the body of Garda Phil Keane was removed from the scene. George asked one of them as to what had happened. A lone fire-engine looked out of place at the top of the street by what was left of Saint Vincent's. George walked up towards the church, half afraid about what he might find. The firemen were still hosing down the smouldering ruins. The pungent smell of burning hung in the air. It was a bizarre sight indeed, with charred timbers and fallen masonry and roof slates scattered and broken among the old gravestones. The revered place of worship was more like a bombsite now or was it a taste of Armageddon?

George regarded the smouldering ruins, aware that the fume laden air was settling on his clothes. He blessed himself and turned to go back to the hotel. As he did, he thought he saw old Mick from the bar standing there among the ruins. But when he glanced at the spot again, old Mick or whoever it was had gone or vanished. He seemed to disappear into thin air, if indeed it was old Mick.

The receptionist beckoned to George as he walked into the foyer of the hotel.

"A lady in room ten would like to see you, Mr Murray. "

He nodded, aware that once again he was coming back into the hotel, after a sleepless night and looking like death warmed up. He took each step of the carpeted stairs, slowly, pensively. He went along the short corridor and knocked on room ten. Lisa opened the door and just stood there unable to say anything and by now George himself was too tired and lost for words.

"You look awful." Lisa eventually said, moving to touch his face but before she could, George rebuffed her advance.

"It's a long story." He said.

Lisa invited him into the room, and he did step inside but not before showing some reluctance. Lisa sat on the end of the bed while George stood several feet away by the window.

"I see you crashed your car but obviously you're ok."

Lisa shook her head. "No, I didn't crash it. Some youngsters stole it shortly after I arrived. I thought you might have been here last night." She said, dismissing the car talk.

It was one of those encounters where the awkward silences, interspersed with trivia, said it all. George kept looking out through the window.

"Terrible fire here last night." He said. "Parish priest was killed."

"I know." She said. "Look George .... I can't excuse ...."

George shook his head. "No, don't. Don't say anything."

Another long silence froze the space between them as he avoided looking at her.

"Why did you come?" He eventually said. "It's no good you know."

"Can you not even try to forgive me?"

"It's not a question of forgiveness." Said George, shaking his head. "It just doesn't matter anymore. There are other things for me to consider now and we're just going to have to get over each other."

Lisa sobbed at hearing George's harsh words which had a desolating finality about them, and she knew that her tears would make no impression. George moved towards the bedroom door, touching her shoulder as he stepped by her.

"I'm sorry." He said as he opened the door and stepped out of the room leaving Lisa to her sobbing.

* * *

George slept soundly until sometime in the afternoon. The cuts to his face weren't as bad as he had thought. Just a few scratches, he observed as he manoeuvred the razor around them. After a shower and with fresh clothes and he was almost ready.

George stepped out onto the Ballynamarbh Main Street. The Garda and fire brigade activity had died down now, leaving a few curious onlookers peering at the smouldering ruins of the church. Deep in thought, he looked across the street towards the Garda station. His conscience was bothering him, as it had been doing, on and off, since that day, a lifetime ago when he was just a boy playing cowboys and Indians with his pals.

His mind was playing games with him now. Should he surrender himself to the authorities and let them settle on justice or should he just leave what is history to history and walk away?

Children's books by Glenn McLernon
Rhyming picture stories with an environmental theme
Ages 4 to 8 years

The Raindance
The Raindrops
The Raindrops: Down the Drain
The Raindrops: On the River
The Raindrops: In the Bay
The Raindrops: Snow Dance

Readers for children aged 6 to 10 years

Pip and Paul: The Little Orphans
Pip and Paul: Christmas Story
Pip and Paul: The Mischievous Shoes

Glenn McLernon
gmclernon@googlemail.com
www.facebook.com/puddlepiddlediddle
Phone 07503184650 (UK)